DAR

Grace and Gumbo

CONTEMPORARY SHORT
STORIES: A COLLECTION FOR
THE MODERN READER

outskirts
press

Grace and Gumbo
Contemporary Short Stories: A Collection for the Modern Reader
All Rights Reserved.
Copyright © 2025 Darren Howard
v1.0

This is a work of fiction. Names, characters, businesses, places, events, locales, and incidents are either the products of the author's imagination or used in a fictitious manner. Any resemblance to actual persons, living or dead, or actual events is purely coincidental.

The opinions expressed in this manuscript are solely the opinions of the author and do not represent the opinions or thoughts of the publisher. The author has represented and warranted full ownership and/or legal right to publish all the materials in this book.

This book may not be reproduced, transmitted, or stored in whole or in part by any means, including graphic, electronic, or mechanical without the express written consent of the publisher except in the case of brief quotations embodied in critical articles and reviews.

Outskirts Press, Inc.
http://www.outskirtspress.com

ISBN: 978-1-9772-7830-2

Outskirts Press and the "OP" logo are trademarks belonging to Outskirts Press, Inc.

PRINTED IN THE UNITED STATES OF AMERICA

Preface

Welcome to a collection of short stories penned by a distinctive voice within the rich tapestry of African American literature. In this anthology, the narratives unfold like notes in a soulful melody, each story resonating with the echoes of a unique cultural heritage. Through the lens of this African American author, we are invited into worlds that blend the universal human experience with the nuances of a specific and vibrant cultural identity.

These short stories are more than literary offerings; they are windows into the complexities of life as seen through the eyes of the African American community. Themes of resilience, heritage, identity, and the diverse spectrum of human relationships weave through the pages. As we embark on this literary journey, we encounter characters who navigate the challenges of their existence with grace, humor, and an enduring spirit.

May these stories not only entertain but also enlighten, offering readers a deeper understanding of the diverse narratives within the African American experience. This collection is a celebration of storytelling that transcends boundaries, and as you immerse yourself in these narratives, may you find moments of reflection, connection, and a celebration of the rich tapestry of African American life and culture.

I'm Sick

After five years since Abram and I separated and ultimately divorced, it wouldn't be truthful if I said I never think about him, but those moments are few and far between. In those five years, I repackaged my life. I decided to go back to college and finish my degree. The pursuit and accomplishment of getting my degree filled a void in my life that Abram had left.

During class, my mind would sometimes wander into the lane of regret. I regret how I put my life on hold, as well as my dreams, for this man. This was something I swore I would never do, but much of my stubbornness was formed in my mind as a young bride. The false bravado of what I will and will not do for a man was quick to come out of my mouth, but life isn't always that easy.

It had always been my dream to be involved in education. I loved children, and since I had none of my own, the thought of being a teacher brought me even more joy. I was without children not because of any medical matters but simply because Abram didn't want to be bogged down with the responsibility that goes along with being a parent. During those five years of separation, I was able to earn my degree, fulfilling my dream of being a teacher. My life was so different in that five-year span that Abram had become nothing but a distant memory. That is until today.

In the middle of teaching class and having a wonderful day with my students, there came a pause in teaching because there was an announcement over the public address system. The voice of the school principal rang out, "Miss Cooper, please report to the Principal's office."

For the life of me, I was clueless as to why I would be needed in the office. I put away my chalk and asked the teacher across the hallway from my class to keep an eye on my students until I returned. As I walked the long hallway to get to the principal's office, my mind started to race. I could not imagine why the Principal would need to see me in the middle of a school day. I could feel my pace picking up, and I started to rub my hands in a nervous gesture.

Upon entering the Principal's office, I was dismayed by what I saw. There was Abram, standing there exchanging small talk with the ladies in the office. I looked toward the Principal with a questioning look, inquiring why I was summoned and what Abram was doing here. The Principal pointed at Abram and then looked at me, saying, "Miss Cooper, I had no idea that you were married. This gentleman stated that he is your husband and urgently needs to speak with you."

I pointed at Abram with disgust and frustration etched across my face and said in my most stern voice, "Will you meet me outside, please!"

Abram pulled himself away from entertaining the ladies in the office, and we made our way to the outside courtyard. "Abram, what on God's green earth are you doing here? How did you know where I work, and who told you that I work here?"

Abram looked at me with a sheepish look. Usually, he would be quick with his words, and he would never put up with me questioning him in such a manner. He put his head down as if he was a defeated champion and uttered, "I'm sick." I heard his words clearly, but I was consumed with my feelings of frustration and anger. Five years had passed without hearing from him, and now he shows up, stating that he is sick.

I tried to put my feelings on the backburner for a moment and inquired about his illness. Abram told me that he has cancer, and it is advanced. The doctors are not giving him much time, and he states that he needs a favor. I am shocked by this news because Abram was always an active, athletic guy. He stayed at the gym working out, and that was one of the issues that led to the end of our marriage. He was consumed by his body image, and when he wasn't working out, he could be found in the bed of any and every young woman he could bat his eyes at.

I turned to Abram and reached out to hold his hand because he was visibly upset. I could see the uncertainty all over his face. Abram said, "Hey, I need a favor, and I know I have no right to ask this of you. I have nowhere to live. The woman I was living with panicked when I told her about my cancer, and she asked me to leave her house. As of today, I have no residence. I wanted to know if you would attend my doctor's visits with me and possibly allow me to live in your house. I promise I will not interfere with your life, and if you have a man, I promise not to get in the way. I just need a peaceful place to lay my head and finish out this life."

I took a step backward and unloaded five years of frustration and anger. "You want to live with me, and you want me to attend your doctor's visits with you? Are you serious right now?"

I had to quickly compose myself because my voice was starting to carry, and I knew the people in the Principal's office would be able to hear me. I looked Abram in the eyes and continued my response but with a lower tone to my voice. "Abram, you have the gall to come to my job and drop this news on me, and now you want me to be some sort of faithful forgiving wife who rescues you in your last days. You should have thought about this five years ago when you were running the streets and chasing every miniskirt you could. You neglected me and ignored our marriage vows. You filed for divorce, telling me how boring and usual I was. You tried to destroy my humanity and crush my self-worth, and now you want some sort of sympathy from me? That train left the station five years ago in the lawyer's office, and since then my life is different. I have a life that centers on me and my needs and has not etched out any room for you. I really am sad that you're sick, but you can't just pop up like this and expect me to welcome you back with open arms!"

Abram looked dejected, a look I had never seen on him before. He was defeated, and it seemed like his last hope was me agreeing to help him in his last days. There was a measure of guilt because he was sick, but it took me five years to get to the point of operating like a real human and not a perpetually wounded woman. I simply could not put my life in reverse and go back to being consumed with Abram Cooper.

I turned toward Abram and gave him a hug. I whispered in his ear, "I am really sorry to hear this news. I will pray for you and I will check up on you from time to time, but I can't have you living with me, and I can't be your caretaker going back and forth to doctor's appointments. I know what I am saying may not sit well with you, but I can't do this again. I hope you understand."

With those words, I watched as Abram walked away. I headed back to my classroom. There were hundreds of thoughts running through my head, but the main thing I needed to concentrate on was my kids. "Okay, kids, everyone calm down, and let's open our books to page nineteen."

The Old Man and the Old Woman

The old woman waited, her anticipation growing as she listened for the familiar sound of the old man's truck pulling into the carport. That sound had become a comforting presence in her life, a dependable marker of his return. As his truck rumbled closer, she imagined him peering out of the window, checking if the warm glow of the kitchen light spilled out into the dusk. Of course, it always did, because she made it a habit to be in the kitchen, a steady presence awaiting his arrival after his day of work.

Retirement had beckoned him from his offshore labor, but idleness was never his calling. Instead, he embraced a new chapter, venturing into self-employment. Financial necessity was not the driving force, but rather the need to engage his active mind and capable hands. This endeavor provided him with purpose, a way to fill his hours constructively.

In the meantime, while the old man toiled away, the old woman pursued her own routines. She faithfully attended her church meetings and embarked on her grocery store errands. Such was her regularity that the store clerks came to recognize her well, striking up conversations about her culinary plans for the day. Amused by this, the old woman would respond with a smile, "I'm still deciding. You know, the other day the old man mentioned his craving for collard greens. And I noticed those pork chops on sale – might just surprise him with some perfectly fried pork chops."

With these daily rhythms and shared considerations, the old couple continued to find their contentment in the ebb and flow of their lives.

Down every aisle of the store, the old woman would venture, her mind occupied with thoughts of what culinary delight she could conjure for the old man. There was a certain satisfaction in knowing that he appreciated her efforts, never once turning his nose up at her dishes. Whatever she prepared, he savored with genuine delight. Once the meal concluded, he'd take the time to carefully wash his plate, leaving it on the rack to dry. A warm embrace and heartfelt words would follow, as he affectionately thanked her, "Dear old woman, this meal was more than nourishment—it was a gift. Thank you for tending to this old man's heart through his stomach."

As the day wound down, the old man would retire to the bathroom for a shower, then bow his head in prayer before sliding beneath the covers. Gratitude for the old woman was a constant in his evening prayers, his words whispered earnestly, thanking the Lord for the companionship and sustenance she provided. Meanwhile, the old woman's own nightly routine differed slightly, as she lingered in solitude a little longer, engrossed in her Bible's teachings. Her prayers would weave a tapestry of thanks, expressing her deep appreciation for the old man who had become the anchor of her life.

Their journey had been far from smooth, marked by years of turbulence that once seemed insurmountable. The old man, in his younger days, was known for his escapades through the streets and his association with other women. The old woman had her own shadowed history, frequently seen at the gambling house, her presence a fixture at the poker table, accompanied by a glass of gin within arm's reach. But time had woven its own magic, mending the tears in their bond and softening the edges of their pasts.

With the passage of countless years and the trials that accompanied them, the old couple had finally found solace in each other's presence. The old man's roving tendencies had transformed into steadfast devotion, and the old woman's vices had evolved into deep, meaningful connection. In the embrace of their enduring love, they had discovered a contentment that eluded them in their earlier days.

The passage of time was not without its share of trials. Many nights were consumed by heated arguments and bitter fights, some escalating to the point where the idea of parting ways loomed ominously. Despite the tempestuous nature of their relationship, an unexplainable force seemed to anchor the old man and the old woman to each other. While the specter of separation often cast its shadow, they persevered, weathering the storm together.

The old man's earlier tendencies to roam the streets and seek solace in other women had dwindled, in part due to the old woman's unwavering presence and the futility of the promises he had once whispered to his extramarital companions. Hollow vows of leaving the old woman and creating a new life had lost their allure, as the old man recognized the depth of his commitment, even amidst their disagreements.

Parallel to this transformation, the old woman found her own dissatisfaction with her former habits. The thrill of shuffling cards and rolling dice gradually waned, and even the taste of gin seemed to have lost its appeal. The once exhilarating victories in card games lost their shine, and a shared weariness of the street life began to unite them.

Subtle changes began to permeate their lives. The old man ceased his visits to the barroom, opting instead for the comfort of home. Likewise, the old woman took a step back from her gambling comrades, announcing her intention to return to the old man and assess whether the love that had brought them together still held true.

With the passage of time, their lives started to orbit around each other's needs and desires. The old woman found fulfillment in her church activities and the simple pleasure of grocery shopping. The old man's sense of purpose flourished as he pursued his self-employment endeavors, and he occasionally indulged in surprising the old woman with a gracefully chosen dress, a small gesture that brought a touch of elegance to her church outings.

This new phase in their journey was a testament to the resilience of their bond, a love that had weathered the storms of their past and evolved into a source of stability and contentment in their present.

Three O'clock in the Morning

It has been a long day, one of those days where you can't wait to get a shower and slip under the covers. I had that day today – stress on the job and stress in my love life. All I want to do is eat a comforting meal, get in bed, and let sleep take over me. These moments of deep rest are some of the best episodes of peace I can get, and I always feel better after I wake up. Tonight is no different.

I doze off, and immediately, I find myself in a dream state. I am not dreaming of anything special – just far-off places and random thoughts that have been stored in my mind. In the middle of these dreams of nothingness, I hear a distant sound. It's a sound that has nothing to do with the mixture of thoughts and dreams I was experiencing. It is my doorbell ringing, and I awaken from this mishmash of thoughts and feelings.

The first thing I do is glance at my clock to get an idea of what time it is. It is 3 AM, so I must still be dreaming. How did this doorbell sound enter my dream state? Could someone really be at my door at 3 AM?

As I approach the door to see what is going on, my mind races with thoughts of a possible emergency in the building. Maybe it's that attractive neighbor from the third floor coming down to express her feelings for me. Or perhaps it's a representative with a giant cardboard check, here to inform me that I've won millions of dollars. With these thoughts swirling in my head, I reach the door and cautiously look through the peephole, my heart pounding.

To my utter shock, I am taken aback as I see who is standing outside – it's my ex-wife. I step back in disbelief, rubbing my eyes to make sure I am not still trapped in a dream. But there she is, unmistakably present before me. My emotions tumble as memories flood my mind, and I'm unsure of what to make of this unexpected and emotional encounter.

I take a deep breath, attempting to collect my thoughts and regain my composure. It's early, and I know my coolness factor doesn't fully kick in until after my first cup of coffee, which is still a few hours away. As I slowly open the door, there she is, my ex-wife, looking as beautiful as ever, as if she just had a relaxing spa day.

Trying to muster a mix of annoyance and disgust, I manage to ask her what on earth she's doing at my door at 3 AM. Before I can say anything else, she brushes past me as if I'm invisible and walks right into my apartment. Familiar scenes unfold as she casually drops her purse on the coffee table, just like she used to do when we were married. Her shady smile hints at mischief as she starts to mockingly inspect the place.

With feigned interest, she acts as if she's going to check out the bedroom and then casually asks me about who might be in my bed tonight. Her words are meant to probe, making reference to women from my past – the woman from Africa I dated last year or Tasha, who used to be her hairdresser.

I find myself torn between frustration and nostalgia, unsure of how to react to her sudden intrusion into my life once again. Memories and emotions surge within me, and I'm left grappling with a mix of old feelings and the desire to maintain my independence and privacy.

In my defensive mode, I can't help but wonder how she knows about the women I've been involved with since our divorce. It's still very early in the morning, and my senses haven't fully woken up to deal with this unexpected situation. It occurs to me that one of her girlfriends lives down the hall, and I am convinced that's where she's getting her information. I suspect her questions about other women are merely a diversion tactic to keep me from asking why she's at my apartment at 3 AM.

With sleep still lingering in my eyes and a strong desire to get back to bed, I firmly assert that my bedroom is none of her business. Finally gathering the courage, I confront her directly and ask her the question that's been on my mind since she arrived.

Her response surprises me, as she laughs and comments on how she forgot how corny I can be, but she still finds it cute. She casually explains that she came from the casino and knew my apartment was on her way home. According to her, she got the security gate code from her girlfriend who lives down the hall. That same girlfriend also informed her that I had been seen alone for the past week, so she was confident I wouldn't have anyone in my bed.

The mix of frustration and confusion intensifies as I try to process her explanation. Part of me wants to challenge her reasons for showing up uninvited, while another part is tempted to reminisce about the past and the unique connection we once had. But before I can say anything else, she continues speaking, leaving me in a whirlwind of emotions and thoughts.

As my initial shock begins to subside, I gather the courage to ask her directly why she is here. A part of me wonders if this could be one of those late-night visits for old times' sake, seeking a late-night connection as we once had. Her response catches me off guard – she wanted to stop by because she heard I was doing well for myself and she wanted to see it firsthand.

She continues sharing her thoughts, mentioning how she believed the divorce would crush me and that she expected to find a broken man living with his mother. Meanwhile, she seems to be making herself quite at home, casually kicking off her shoes and even rummaging through my refrigerator to warm up some leftover red beans on the stove. My mind is still trying to grasp the reason for her surprise visit; the time of morning is no longer a factor – I'm just genuinely mystified as to why she's here.

As she relaxes in the kitchen, memories of our past flood my mind, reminding me of the nights we used to cook together and how she effortlessly exuded a captivating charm. It's not in a male chauvinistic way, but rather, there was a magnetic allure about her, and everything she did seemed to carry an air of sensuality. Despite my confusion, I can't help but notice how good she looks, and her presence evokes a mix of emotions.

While she goes on about her experience at the casino and how the slot machines aren't paying out, my mind is momentarily captivated by the nostalgia of the past. But deep down, questions still linger about the true motive behind her unexpected visit.

As I shout in frustration, putting a pause to her rambling, I can't help but express my bewilderment at the situation. I ask her directly what exactly is going on – her unexpected visit, acting as if it's completely normal, sitting on my sofa, warming up food, and seemingly making herself at home. I even throw in a hint of sarcasm, jokingly questioning if she's planning to jump into my bed and hog all the covers as she used to do during our marriage. My emotions are swirling, and I can't help but wonder if this is some bizarre episode from a bad movie, where the divorce never happened and everything is a dream.

Her smile in response to my outburst catches me off guard, and she calmly reminds me that she doesn't appreciate being yelled at. She tries to explain that she had been concerned about me and wanted to see for herself how I was doing. According to her, the divorce was hard on me, and her visit was motivated by genuine concern. She brings up seeing me at several Pelicans games with different dates, and it appears she's questioning my recent dating behavior, wondering if I might be going through a midlife crisis.

I listen to her words, taking in the reminders of the last year of our marriage and the pain that it brought, particularly with the suspicions of an affair. It's clear that emotions are still raw between us, and our history is coming back to the surface in this unexpected reunion.

As she continues to speak, I try to process everything she's saying, from her concern about my well-being to her observations about my dating life. My mind races, torn between feelings of frustration, nostalgia, and a hint of defensiveness. Deep down, I know that this impromptu visit is stirring up old wounds and unresolved emotions, leaving me in a state of confusion about how to react to her presence once again.

As the conversation continues, I notice a momentary look of shame in her eyes, but she still doesn't admit to any infidelity during our marriage. I assure her that my life is indeed good, and I have the freedom to date whoever I want, whenever I want. While I reflect on our past, I can't help but wonder if things went sour because I was unable to provide her with the finer things in life, although she knew the situation before we got married.

Perhaps it was a combination of youth and unfulfilled expectations on both our parts. I had accepted that my life was destined to be normal, with the usual struggles of making ends meet and dealing with bills that sometimes become overwhelming. I acknowledge how life often revolves around money, and financial issues are a common reason for couples to split.

Interestingly, the divorce wasn't about our lack of money, at least not directly. However, it seems that her perspective changed when she met someone who had an abundance of wealth. Suddenly, a life of financial abundance made the life we had together seem insufficient in comparison. It's a common human tendency – once you have a lot, even a little can feel like too little.

As we both reflect on the past and its complexities, I realize that perhaps our paths had to diverge to find greater happiness and fulfillment in different ways. Our relationship was a learning experience, and we both grew from it, even if it meant going our separate ways. It's a bittersweet realization that life has its twists and turns, and sometimes it takes encountering other possibilities to realize what truly brings us contentment and joy.

As she listens to me, she admits that she never wanted us to be apart, and her vulnerability shows through as she recounts the first time she saw me with another woman. Despite being with her new wealthy husband, she confesses that she excused herself from his company and wept in the ladies' room. Her emotions were raw, and she shares that my reaction to her at that moment felt cold and distant, but she understands that it came in the aftermath of a blindsiding divorce.

She opens up about how going to the movies together was our date night routine, and witnessing me sharing that experience with another woman was deeply hurtful. As she shares these feelings, I find myself feeling sorry for the pain she went through, even though we were already separated at that point.

However, the weight of the conversation and the time of the early morning begin to affect me, and I notice that it's approaching 4 AM. I kindly ask her to leave, as I need some rest and the walk down memory lane has been emotionally taxing. But she reminds me that it's Saturday morning and that I don't work on weekends. Her presence and the depth of our conversation make it challenging for me to stand firm in asking her to leave.

As she dishes her food and invites me to join her, I hesitate and decline her offer, mentioning that I have plastic containers to pack the food. But her smile, that same captivating smile that captured my heart years ago, softens my resolve once again. I find myself torn between past emotions and the need to set boundaries for my own well-being.

In this complex moment, I'm reminded of the history we share and the profound impact we've had on each other's lives. However, I also recognize that it's essential to prioritize self-care and maintain clear boundaries to navigate this unexpected reunion.

As she opens up about her current situation with her wealthy husband, she explains that money can sometimes feel like a fleeting illusion – here one moment, gone the next. She reveals that despite the lavish lifestyle they lead with an expensive house in River Ridge and luxury cars, it comes with its own set of challenges, including infidelity and sleepless nights.

She shares candidly about her husband's long road trips and late-night meetings, which often lead to him coming home with evidence of his indiscretions, like lipstick on his collar. This stark contrast to how discreetly I handled any attraction to other women during our marriage stands out to her.

Her husband's behavior is unapologetically blatant, even to the point of making her feel jealous and inadequate, while dismissing her feelings as a consequence of his fame. She bravely admits that his jealousy over her looking at other men has led to fits of rage and even physical abuse.

It's evident that our conversation is evoking a mix of emotions in her, and she lets out words that she may have kept hidden, speaking about the domestic violence she has experienced. The vulnerability in her voice shows how complicated and distressing her current situation is.

Despite the challenges she faces, she admits that she still smiles when our song comes on the radio, a nostalgic reminder of the connection we once shared. In contrast, she doesn't have a song with her current husband, as he prefers a different type of music that doesn't hold the same sentimental value.

As she finishes her meal and places the bowl in the sink, a sense of quiet settles between us. I find myself speechless, unsure of how to respond to the unexpected turn of events. I had believed that divorcing me was what she truly wanted, and marrying a professional ball player would fulfill her dreams. But her visit and her candid revelations have shattered those assumptions.

As she grabs her purse from the coffee table, she surprises me once again by pulling me into a hug. Her whispered words in my ear touch my heart and leave me in a state of emotional turmoil. She thanks me for loving her, acknowledging that it was because of me that she experienced what real love is, or perhaps what it once was.

With those final words, she heads toward the door and leaves, and I'm left standing there, trying to make sense of the encounter that just transpired. The clock now reads almost 5 AM, and I'm left feeling a mix of emotions – confusion, nostalgia, and a tinge of sadness. I know that she won't divorce her current husband or come back to me. This is the reality of life, where not all endings are happy and where people make decisions about the lives they want to lead.

As she leaves, I am forced to accept that our paths have diverged, and we are both moving forward with our lives in different directions. It's a bittersweet realization, but I also recognize that I am content with the life I have now, and sometimes life leads us down unexpected paths. As I reflect on our history and what we once shared, I find solace in knowing that I was able to experience and give real love, even if it took us on separate journeys in the end.

Five Minutes

Waiting is something I have never been good at. My mother used to tell me that I was impatient, that I would not let her go through birth pangs like other mothers. I insisted on coming straight out of her womb. Now, I find myself waiting, and my palms are sweaty, and my throat is dry. I think to myself, "Why can't we just get this over with?" But I know you can't rush some things.

I have been background-checked by everyone in Washington D.C., as if I were the President himself, instead of a guest of the President. The Secret Service has spoken to everyone, from my preacher to my tax man, inquiring about me. They have even spoken with my mother and worried her, as if I were on some Most Wanted List. All this for a simple visit to the White House. But then again, what is simple about such a visit?

I am here not because I am some political figure, but as a reward for hard work and endurance. My students submitted my name for Teacher of the Year in a contest that measures teachers throughout the nation. I teach middle school kids in a makeshift school in post-Katrina New Orleans. Our school is still under repair from years ago, and at times I wonder if the structure will hold up over our heads. But we show up every day and fight on. We fight against ignorance and despair in a city where despair can take hold of a person in no time. We fight against crushed dreams, even though our kids see many crushed dreams as they walk the streets of New Orleans toward their schoolhouse.

Our school is dedicated to hope in the midst of a sometimes hopeless city, but a city that, at its core, is about love and tradition. I am humbled to be selected as Teacher of the Year because I don't believe in great teachers; I believe in great students. My dreams of riches and fame were dashed among the levees of the 9th ward, and my life turned around due to the aftermath.

I left my dreams of a career in business to turn to the education of the youth in our city. I dreaded the scenes of despair and violence that appeared on our television screens at night, and I decided to do something about it. I made my way into the educational system with a determination to make a difference in my city by making a difference in our youth.

Now, I sit in a white-washed room in the White House, a room that they very seldom show on television, and I wait. I am here with other Teachers of the Year, and I am sure we all share a passion for what we do and how we do it. I am surprised that there is so little conversation between the educators of the year, but I think all of us are nervous. I can see it in our eyes and in our body language as we sit and show signs of nervousness. One teacher wipes her brow as perspiration gathers on her forehead. Another teacher nervously bites his fingernails as if he is waiting for his first date to arrive. I glance at another teacher who constantly adjusts his tie, making sure it is in its proper place. We are all leaders and educators gathered in one room, but we are also humans, showing signs of nervousness.

The Secret Service agent comes into the room one last time to tell us that the President will be with us shortly and gives us last-minute instructions on what to do and what not to do. We all glance over our shoulders as one teacher jokes and asks what will happen if we don't follow the instructions. The young Secret Service agent ignores the joke and continues with a straight face, delivering stern instructions. We all take our seats once again and wait.

As I wait once again, I think back to my mother and wonder if she is looking down from Heaven right now. I wonder if she is proud of her young boy who would have never thought of being a teacher but wanted to be a cowboy. Will she remember the days when I talked about leaving New Orleans and moving to the West to work on a ranch and ride horses? Will she smile from Heaven to see her son dressed in a suit and tie for a happy occasion and not for a funeral? I want her to be the proudest mother in Heaven as she and the angels look down upon me at this moment.

Just as I am lost in my own thoughts, the door opens, and in walk a few Secret Service agents. This time they have someone behind them, and we all stand to our feet. In walks the President of the United States, and the magnitude of the moment hits me like a block of concrete. My palms are sweating, and I am hoping that he doesn't want to shake my hand right now because he will get a palm full of moisture.

He is taller than I imagined, and he has a presence about him that goes beyond description. He seems so different from the candidate I watched on television who fought so hard against the naysayers of the opposite party. He seems to be a man not at war against his opponents but a man at peace with his place in the world. He has a calmness about him and a way of smiling that says he is a man of authority but also a man who has a heart.

We are given a final instruction to stand in a line and wait for him to greet us one by one. There will be no individual pictures, only a staff photographer who will take a group picture at the end. The President makes his way down the line of teachers and shakes our hands one by one, calling us by our first names as if he has always known us. He speaks to us in a way that would suggest he was once one of our students or an old friend.

We were given instructions not to make sudden moves toward him, but to let him initiate all movements. That was made clear to us in our meeting, and yet a young teacher reaches out to hug him with tears flowing down her face. The President reacts by giving her a warm, heartfelt hug as the young Secret Serviceman inches forward in case this hug turns into a security issue. The President consoles this woman, and they exchange words that only they can hear as he looks her in the eyes and comforts her soul. The young Secret Serviceman looks at me with a look that says I better not step out of line, and I get his message immediately. The President will soon be in front of me, and the moment is very near. Once again, my palms are moist, and my leg starts to shake. I haven't been this nervous since my fourth-grade girlfriend gave me a candy bar and said she wanted me to be her boyfriend.

The President makes his way to stand in front of me, and with a firm handshake, he shakes my hand and says he is proud of me and the work I am doing. With a dry mouth and a smile on my face that eventually would hurt my cheeks, I nod and say something that was meant to be "thank you" but comes out in moans that could be mistaken for a foreign language. The President takes his left hand and firmly places it on my shoulder and looks me in the eye one last time before moving on to the next teacher. I feel like the little boy from New Orleans who dreamed of being a cowboy but is now a grown man. I think of my mother again, and I wonder what she would think at this very moment, and I begin to tear up. Just as I tear up, I catch myself and gather my emotions. The young Secret Serviceman comes over and instructs us to gather together for a photo opportunity. The President stands in the middle of the group, and we surround him and all glare into the camera as the photographer snaps several pictures.

In the midst of one of the most glorious moments of my life, I hear a voice from behind the group telling us to wrap it up because the President has a meeting. I think to myself, what could be his next meeting? Could it be a meeting with a world leader, or could it be another meeting with the opposite party? I look at my watch, and in a little more than five minutes, my level of inspiration has been uplifted even higher than ever before. I get ready to wrap up my visit and return to New Orleans with more fire in my loins for my city and for teaching. One five-minute visit has changed my life from the inside, even though I am returning to a city torn up on the outside. I know in the years to come that the President will probably not remember that I was one of the best teachers of that year, but I will never forget him or my visit.

Fond Farewell

"Today marks the end of an incredible journey, one that I never imagined would come so soon – the day of my retirement. Looking back on the day I was drafted, I couldn't have fathomed the highs and lows, the triumphs and challenges that would come to define my career. As I stand here before you, I can't help but feel a mix of emotions – nostalgia for the days on the field, gratitude for the support of fans like you, and excitement for the future that lies ahead.

Throughout my career, I've been incredibly fortunate to have achieved what some might consider a Hall of Fame career. But let me tell you, it wasn't just about the accolades or the statistics. It was about the passion for the game, the camaraderie with my teammates, and the love and dedication of the fans that fueled my every move."

At times like these, athletes often read from scripted statements, carefully crafted to evoke the right emotions and responses. But today, I want to break free from that mold. For the first time in my public life, I want to be genuine and speak from the heart.

"In my years as a professional ballplayer, and even during my college days, I must admit that I wasn't always honest with you all. I played it safe, giving the "right" responses to questions, fearing the repercussions of speaking my mind. It's true that we, as public figures, are often conditioned to be guarded and politically neutral. But looking back, I regret not having the courage to be more authentic.

So, today, I stand here to tell you that I am human. I've had moments of doubt, times of exhaustion, and struggles with the immense pressure that comes with being in the spotlight. I wish I had been more forthcoming about those moments, for it is through our vulnerabilities that we truly connect with one another.

Beyond the cheers of the crowds and the adrenaline of competition, there's a part of me that is eager to give back to the sport that has given me so much. I look forward to exploring opportunities in the administrative aspect of the game. Whether it's through coaching, mentoring young athletes, or contributing to the development of the sport, I want to remain connected to the essence of what makes this game so special.

To my fellow retirees, I know that each of us will choose our own paths after stepping away from the field. Some will find solace in television, others will become ambassadors and marketers of the sport, while a few might retreat to a life of relative anonymity. No matter the choice, I wish my fellow athletes nothing but success and fulfillment in their post-playing careers.

And so, as I step into the next phase of my life, I carry with me the valuable lessons learned from this sport – dedication, resilience, and teamwork. I may no longer wear the jersey, but the spirit of the game will always be a part of me.

Thank you all for being here today, and thank you for allowing me to be honest and genuine for once. It means more to me than you'll ever know."

To the fans,

It's with a heavy heart that I address you today, reflecting on what was once a beautiful relationship between us. You cheered for me, and in return, I gave you my all on the field night after night. Your support meant the world to me, and it often inspired me to push through injuries and give my best for the team and for you.

However, somewhere along the way, our relationship took a painful turn, and it became clear that we were headed down a road of division and hostility. I couldn't ignore the shift from mutual respect to what felt like total abuse. It hurt deeply to experience the way some of you reacted when I didn't perform up to your expectations.

I remember a particularly difficult moment during my rookie year when I had to sit out a playoff game due to an infection. The yelling and obscenities hurled at me from the stands were disheartening, especially when children were present. It made me wonder what example was being set for the next generation.

As a public figure, I've come to accept that my personal life will be under scrutiny to some extent. However, I never anticipated the level of intrusion and disrespect I experienced from some fans. It was difficult to enjoy a simple evening with my family without being interrupted for autographs and pictures. While I cherished your support, there were times when I needed space to be a father and husband.

The requests for inappropriate autographs and the lack of consideration for my family's presence were deeply upsetting. No one should be subjected to such uncomfortable situations, and it's disheartening to think that some fans felt entitled to treat me that way because they supported me on the field.

Furthermore, the invasion of my personal life reached a new low when private photos were shared with the media, tarnishing my marriage. The woman in those photos was a family member, not an affair partner, yet the accusations and judgment persisted. It was a painful and unjust ordeal for my family.

Even during times of immense grief, some of you crossed boundaries that should never be crossed. I'll never forget how you treated me during my mother's funeral, asking for group photos in front of her casket. It was a moment of profound sorrow and vulnerability, and your actions added to the pain.

I want to emphasize that athletes are human beings too. We have feelings, families, and personal lives beyond the sport we love. It's essential to remember that our success on the field doesn't entitle anyone to invade our personal space or disrespect us as individuals.

I don't harbor ill will towards anyone, but I hope that my story serves as a reminder to treat athletes and public figures with kindness, empathy, and understanding. We are more than just players; we are fathers, mothers, sons, daughters, and friends.

I want to express my gratitude to the fans who have supported me with genuine respect and love throughout my career. Your encouragement has meant the world to me, and I will forever cherish the positive memories we shared.

As I step away from the game, I hope that we can all learn from these experiences and move towards a more compassionate and respectful sports culture. Thank you for being a part of my journey, and I wish you all the best.

Today, as I bid farewell to my career, I feel compelled to address something that has been weighing heavily on my conscience. It's time to come clean about a truth that has been hidden for far too long.

To my agent,

Throughout my entire career, Jack Ford has been my agent, starting from my college days. I know this revelation may come as a shock to many, considering college athletes are not supposed to have agents. But the reality is that Jack has been involved in my life since I was a freshman in college. He started by offering me gifts and money, and over time, his involvement escalated to arranging various other benefits, including academic assistance and relationships with women.

At the time, Jack convinced me that I deserved compensation because my college was profiting immensely from my talent. He made it seem like I was just getting my fair share of the revenue. While I knew deep down that we were breaking the rules, I went along with it, trusting Jack's justifications.

What I didn't fully realize then was the extent to which Jack was exploiting not only me but also many other athletes. He made millions off the backs of athletes while constantly reminding us that we owed him our success. It was a toxic relationship built on manipulation and control.

One significant incident that truly opened my eyes was when I discovered that Jack was hindering potential endorsement opportunities for me. He refused to approach certain companies, claiming I wasn't the right fit for their image. However, it turned out that he was secretly directing those opportunities to another client of his.

This blatant betrayal of trust shattered any remaining loyalty I had towards Jack. His actions made me question if he ever had my best interests at heart or if it was all about his personal gains.

So, today, I want to make it clear that I am severing all ties with Jack Ford. I will no longer work with someone who manipulates and stifles my potential for their benefit. My fellow athletes, if you're listening, I urge you to be cautious and vigilant when it comes to your agents. Make sure you have someone who genuinely has your best interests at heart and not just their own bottom line.

To the companies and sponsors out there, if you have ever been misled by Jack's claims about me or any other athlete, I apologize. Please understand that we are not all complicit in these actions, and some of us have been victims of his schemes as well.

As I step into the next phase of my life, I promise to be true to myself and to uphold the values that this sport has taught me. Integrity, honesty, and fairness will guide my actions from here on out.

Thank you to all the fans who have supported me throughout my career. Your unwavering belief in me has meant the world, and I hope to continue making a positive impact in whatever path I choose to pursue.

To The Media

As I stand before you on this momentous day of my retirement, I am filled with a mix of emotions. There is something I must address, a truth that has burdened me throughout my career, and now is the time to speak my mind.

The media, you have been a constant presence in my life, and it hasn't always been easy to navigate this relationship. From the very beginning, you portrayed me in a way that perpetuated stereotypes, focusing on my physical attributes rather than acknowledging my hard work, dedication, intelligence, and leadership skills. While you hailed my teammates for their talents and skills, you often overlooked my contributions that extended beyond the playing field.

You labeled me as a role model, even after I expressed that I only wished to be a role model for my own children. It was never my responsibility to be the role model for the entire world's children, and I struggled with that pressure. Moreover, you twisted my words, turning my honest questions about the perception of Black athletes as role models into accusations of racism.

The media's relentless intrusion into my personal life made it difficult for my children to lead a normal life. You followed them to school, playgrounds, and made their upbringing far from ordinary. You focused on aspects of my life that were meant to uplift, such as my fashion choices, and used them as fodder for ridicule.

Racial references and double standards hurt deeply, making me feel undervalued and disrespected. You placed blame on me for the team's shortcomings, while giving my counterparts praise and understanding in similar situations. This inconsistency only served to fuel the divide.

Yet, as I prepared to deliver this farewell statement, I realized that I have another side to share. Yes, I have faced challenges and injustices, but I have also been blessed with opportunities beyond my wildest dreams. From the humble beginnings in the projects of New Orleans to achieving success as a professional athlete, I have lived a life of which I once only dreamed.

And to the team ownership group, your belief in me and your willingness to invest in my abilities mean more than words can express.

In the end, I have decided to focus on the positive, on the love and gratitude that outweighs the challenges. My journey has been a mixture of ups and downs, and today, I choose to cherish the memories and the people who made it all possible.

Thank you for being part of my story, and as I step into this new chapter of my life, I hope that we can all learn from our experiences and grow together.

Sincerely,
HUMAN

Yuletide

It's that time of the year again, the time when wreaths adorn doors and lights illuminate the eaves and roofs of neighborhood houses. It's a time when kids can hardly get a good night's rest due to their anticipation of finding toys under their trees. It's a time for good food and lots of interior decorations. That's how the world views this time of the year. For me, however, it is a time of sadness.

It has been years since a tragic event soured me on the holidays. We're coming up on exactly six years since Deron was taken from me. Six years ago, we were like many young couples, decorating the interior of our apartment. We hung lights on our balcony and had a list of holiday parties to attend. Like most young couples, we were madly in love and had plans to marry. We were just being patient and what we thought was smart. Deron was working toward his college degree, and I had just finished my commitment to the armed services. We were checking off the boxes of life and aligning them with our plans.

It was six years ago when I received Deron's phone call. He was participating in a study group and wanted me to know he would be running behind. We had plans for an evening dinner at our favorite restaurant. This place was renowned for its stewed okra over rice, a dish I loved because it reminded me so much of my mother's cooking. While Deron wasn't a big eater, he indulged in their bread pudding as often as his waistline would allow. Our plan was to meet there for a relaxing meal and some quality time together. Of course, I knew our conversation would eventually turn to his school work and our future plans.

Occasionally, Deron would bring flyers he had gathered about homes that were for sale. We would dream about one day being able to place a bid on a home of our own. Since leaving the Armed Forces, I had taken a job as a substitute teacher at an elementary school. I could easily see myself going to college to become certified as a teacher for young minds. Becoming a teacher was something that had never crossed my mind before, but working with these kids had been life-changing. It had left such a profound impact on us that one of the boxes we wanted to check off on our life list was becoming parents.

At first, I had apprehensions, but Deron assured me that we would be great parents and a blessing to our kids. Our lives were filled with excitement, with so much of life lying ahead of us. I guess we talked about and planned for our future so much that we lost sight of the present, the here and now.

It was six years ago when I walked into our favorite restaurant, shaking off the excess raindrops from my umbrella. I remember every detail from that night. Hanging up my coat on the restaurant's coat-rack, folding my scarf neatly, and being escorted to a table by the big picture window. I was greeted by our usual server, who asked, "Are you dining alone tonight?"

I remember smiling and telling her that Deron would soon be here, that I was waiting for him to arrive from school. Our server placed her pen and pad in her apron and said, "Let me check with the cooks and see if they have any more bread pudding. Even the cooks know that is what he will order when they see you two together."

As she walked away, I recall looking out the window towards the parking lot and seeing Deron approaching the restaurant. He had on his navy blue pea coat that I had purchased for him the previous holiday and his paperboy cap. I placed the palm of my hand on the window pane so that he could see me from a distance. I wanted him to know that I had secured us a seat, and all he had to do was enter and join me.

I wish I could say that everything ended well, but this night didn't. Deron never made it across the street from the parking lot. While crossing Magazine Street, Deron suffered a massive heart attack. I remember seeing him collapse to one knee and eventually fall flat on the ground. I recall the echo of my screams bouncing off the restaurant's walls as our server dropped two glasses of water. I ran outside to Deron's side, my hand shaking, and my mind racing like it had never raced before.

Someone from the restaurant must have called for help because I could barely speak. I was so focused on holding Deron's hand and assuring him that help was on the way. I remember the look in his eyes, a distant and lifeless look. I refused to believe that this was happening or that he wouldn't be okay. We were young, and this sort of thing doesn't happen to young people. I held Deron's hand and caressed it against my face, wanting him to know that I wasn't going anywhere and that everything would be fine, but that distant look remained on his face.

That night, right before the holiday, is etched in my memory as the night Deron passed away on the cold, wet pavement of Magazine Street. He left this world before help could arrive, and I was left in stunned silence. I couldn't cry or show any emotions. My armed forces training had prepared me for many things, even life-threatening situations, but nothing could have prepared me for that moment. I remember our server bringing out my coat from the coatrack and placing it across my shoulders and hugging me.

That was six years ago, and many sleepless nights have passed since then. I moved on to another relationship, a nice guy who even seemed like the type to marry. However, a big piece of my heart remained on that cold, wet street, and it still feels like it died there that night. I haven't ventured down Magazine Street in six years, and I have no desire to eat at that restaurant again. The memories are too deep and vivid, and I fear it would set me back emotionally.

So now, during this time of the year, I go through the motions. My smiles are hard-fought, as I am inundated with memories. While everyone is busy exchanging gifts and toasting with eggnog, I find myself settling in, trying to keep my mind intact. I understand that life is for the living, and I owe it to my new relationship to be present, but the trauma still washes over me like a sweltering wave. So, I bite my lip and keep moving forward for the sake of the living.

Happy Yuletide.

Race Track

I find myself at this juncture, not entirely sure how I arrived here. The sign prominently displays the visiting hours, but my concern lies beyond those temporal constraints. All I yearn for now is to lay eyes on him. Despite being aware of his recent heart attack, my singular focus is to be by his side. I crave the simple act of holding his hand and gazing into his face. My desire is to whisper reassuring words in his ear, mirroring the comfort he once provided me during moments of childhood anxiety, be it about sports or relationships. His words were a solace, and now, I wish to reciprocate. However, an impediment presents itself in the form of a sign.

Undeterred, I navigate my way to the nurses' station and implore the attending nurse. I repeat my plea tirelessly, emphasizing the considerable effort it took to drive over an hour to reach here. Surely, they cannot deny me the chance to see him. I lay out my predicament before the head nurse, explaining my arduous journey, but her resolve remains unyielding. Behind those resolute eyes, I discern a woman unwaveringly adhering to the rules.

A few hours ago, I received a call from my dad's landlord, informing me that they found him on the floor in pain, clutching at his chest. Initially hesitant to answer the phone, as the landlord typically called only when the rent check was overdue, I braced myself for another round of explanations. Over the past few years, I had taken charge of my dad's financial affairs. It wasn't a matter of his incompetence or absentmindedness, but rather his tendency to prioritize other things over the essentials.

My dad had a deep love for watching horse races. During my childhood, he would drop me off at school and head straight to the race track to indulge in the excitement of watching the ponies run. There were instances when I waited outside of school for him to pick me up, only to realize he wouldn't show up. Knowing the routine, I would make my way to the race track. Like clockwork, I would find him at the bar across the street from the track, immersed in conversation with fellow enthusiasts.

He and his friends would passionately share tales of legendary horses and revered jockeys, emphasizing the bravery and heart these small-statured riders displayed on the racetrack. On most evenings, my intuition proved correct, and I would enter the bar to find him. Despite forgetting to pick me up, he would apologize and attempt to make amends by buying me a soft drink and a bag of potato chips.

I marveled at how he commanded the room, surrounded by friends from the race track, holding court until the sun began to set. However, there were occasions when I would pull up a chair near the kitchen to start on my homework. The bartender, with a hint of disdain, would occasionally gesture towards me, stating, "Hey guys, I'm running a bar here, not an after-school program. Honestly, this kid doesn't belong in a barroom filled with gamblers and alcoholics."

In the face of the bartender's irritation, my dad would dismiss him with a wave, asserting, "Hey, give my kid another soft drink, please, and just let him do his homework. For goodness' sakes, he's not bothering you or your other customers!"

As I sit in the hospital, a profound sense of helplessness washes over me, triggering a cascade of memories. Struggling to control my thoughts, I resist dwelling on the image of him alone in that room. The prospect of his potential demise looms, even though I'm aware that everyone has their appointed time. I find myself unprepared for this reality.

Feeling a profound sense of helplessness, I grapple with the fact that a mere sign and a nurse, who could rival a soldier on duty, stand between me and my dad. Just as I start to succumb to silent panic, my own mind begins to betray me with thoughts of death and finality. It's peculiar how the mind can turn against you in times like this.

Just as I teeter on the edge of a dark mental precipice, a glimmer of hope appears in the form of a young doctor emerging from his room. A radiant expression of joy adorns her face as she halts at the nurses' station for a brief exchange with the head nurse. In the midst of their conversation, the nurse gestures in my direction. The doctor makes her way towards me, and as I rise to hear the news, she extends her hand and delivers reassuring words, "Your father will be fine. He needs some rest, but he was very anxious to tell me what a fine son you are. He even invited me on a date to the race track. I'll override the hour restrictions, allowing you to see him, as long as you don't stay too long and avoid exciting him."

Grateful for the soothing news, I express my thanks to the doctor and prepare myself to see him, hopeful that I can whisper in his ear that everything will be fine.

Empty Space

Words have never been my specialty, especially when they escape my mouth. I was born amidst pain and verbal agony, a fact I've been reminded of countless times. My mother used to recount the excruciating pain she endured during my birth, insisting that my silence as a child was a result of being traumatized by her loud birthing cries. I believed her unquestioningly and never gave it a second thought. I was a child of the mind, not the mouth. On the rare occasions when I did speak, it often turned into a fiasco. I struggled with stuttering, or as my mother would put it, a rush of many words trying to emerge simultaneously. Regardless of the cause, speaking was not my strong suit. So, I made sure to keep my mouth shut and my mind sharp. I could outthink the average person and formulate sentences in my head, but please, Lord, don't ask me to articulate them.

My father had a fondness for saying that words fill the voids or spaces in the atmosphere, and that the atmosphere around me was empty. He insisted that I should speak my mind instead of standing before people with that sheepish grin on my face. I thought he might see the pain etched on my face as my words jumbled up inside my mouth and made a hasty escape, resembling a jailbreak. Would I ever find the ability to express myself in a manner considered normal, or would I remain imprisoned in this struggle? It felt as if my thoughts raced ahead of my words, and at times, people told me that my words were lazy. Just imagine that—my words were deemed lazy. I sought refuge in books and television, immersing myself in the world of possibilities and imagination. I was a child whose words piled up with nowhere to go, so I held them in my mind, allowing them to marinate but not to escape.

I often reminisce about those days when my family would gather around the kitchen table, engaging in lively conversations that covered a spectrum of topics - work, school, education, social issues, politics, and even some neighborhood gossip. I would sit back, filled with wonder, as my brothers and sisters chatted away without any hindrance from their thoughts. It was as though their minds and mouths were in perfect harmony, akin to jazz musicians performing in the clubs of the French Quarters. I eagerly awaited my turn to speak, my mind abuzz with a million thoughts and an abundance of words poised at the gates of my mouth. At the table, I couldn't help but envy the adventurous lives my siblings led, their discussions sounding like the words of great authors or the notes of skilled musicians. Their stories about their days in the world were captivating, and Mother and Father beamed with pride and admiration as they listened.

Eventually, it would come time for me to share about my own life and my experiences in the world. Those were the moments of sheer dread, with my sisters stifling giggles as I struggled to synchronize my thoughts and words. After a few agonizing minutes, my brothers would start clearing their plates, discarding leftover food into the trash can. My mother would find excuses to tidy the table and store away pots in the refrigerator, avoiding eye contact with me as if she wished to conceal her disappointment. She recognized that my brothers and sisters were articulate and well-rounded, seemingly destined for success, but what about me? As I stood there, attempting my best to convey the thoughts swirling in my mind, the only person left at the table would be my father. My father possessed remarkable patience, and the look of disappointment that others displayed was absent in his eyes. Instead, there was an expression of eager anticipation on his face, providing me with the encouragement I needed to make it through each day, from one meal to the next.

I faced the same struggles at school, where my test scores revealed my intelligence, but my words failed to exhibit the same grace. I endured laughter so frequently that I found my place at the back of the classroom, concealing my word-related challenges as far away from the front as possible. To me, the front of the class resembled a stage. Whenever we were called to the blackboard or the teacher's desk, it felt akin to stepping onto the stage of a jazz club. Being called to perform meant not only knowing the answers to the questions posed but also articulating those answers coherently. I had one part of the equation down - I knew most of the answers with ease, but articulation was where I stumbled. It wasn't until my junior year of high school that my prayers seemed to be answered, as a young teacher arrived at my school. He knew nothing of my struggles with words but was well aware of my test scores and my usual spot in the back of the classroom.

On a cold winter day, as I recall, he summoned me to the "stage" as I thought of it. This teacher, who boasted about having taught men who had fought battles in wars, insisted that I release my grip on the chair's arms and make my way to the front. I was called out, front and center, to explain my thoughts on the topic I had written about the day before.

How can I ever forget the agony of walking up to that stage, standing before my peers, and justifying what I had written? How can I ever erase the taste of the experience from my memory, with the kids laughing and giggling, knowing that I was about to put on a comical performance filled with jumbled words? I thought of my own family, how they would discreetly distance themselves from the kitchen table as I took center stage to share my thoughts about my day. I thought of my mother, who would retreat from my thoughts and tangled words, finding solace in storing leftovers in the refrigerator. Somehow, on that day, I summoned the courage to leave all those images behind and approach the stage to discuss my written work. I gathered my resolve and glanced toward my teacher, who wore an expression of anticipation and confidence on his face. I opened my mouth with confidence and poise, knowing exactly what I wanted to talk about. The first words flowed effortlessly, and I felt that, for once in my life, I was on my way to a positive experience with words. However, I can't pinpoint where I went wrong, or maybe it was my eagerness to express myself, but the words became tangled inside my mouth, battling against each other to emerge.

The classroom erupted in laughter, and as I glanced toward the teacher, his once-confident expression had transformed into one of bewilderment. I collected my work and embarked on my journey back to my seat at the back of the classroom. The kids couldn't contain their laughter, and if it weren't for the teacher's reprimand, they might still be chuckling about it today. It was at that moment that I made a solemn vow to myself: I would never attempt to speak again. All my words would remain locked in my mind, never to escape from my mouth.

As the bell rang to dismiss the class, the teacher approached me and asked if I'd be willing to help him grade papers after school. He offered to pay me a modest amount, not enough to make me rich, but sufficient to have a little extra change in my pockets. I discussed the proposal with my father, who saw no harm in me earning a few coins, as long as everything was above board.

Those after-school sessions initially revolved around me assisting the teacher in grading papers but soon evolved into impromptu speaking lessons. We began with lessons he had learned in the military, focusing on how to remain composed and breathe during stressful times. He shared stories of his days in the battle zone and how he had to maintain his composure to lead his men into battle. His memories of fear and intimidation were vivid, as if they had occurred just moments ago, but so were his recollections of how he had conquered that fear.

As I helped grade papers, we practiced his techniques of composure and ensuring that my thoughts aligned with my words. I learned to speak slowly and how to discipline my thoughts within my mind.

I discovered that most people have a multitude of thoughts racing through their minds, but they can corral them and allow them to pass through the gateway of their mouth one by one. My issue, on the other hand, was the opposite - I was attempting to release all my thoughts from the gate of my mouth simultaneously, and I struggled to make them fall in line. Every evening, we diligently worked on honing my thought discipline and ensuring that my words aligned with one thought at a time.

That year became the best of my life as I began to speak in a much clearer manner, with only occasional logjams in my words. With all the hard work and my newfound treasure of words and thoughts aligning, I decided it was time to speak at the dinner table. I had been practicing speaking out loud as I walked from school navigating the cracked sidewalks of Kerlerec Street. I was so excited about my newfound discipline that I wanted to converse with anyone and everyone around me. The neighbors would give me puzzled looks as I spoke to them every evening. Initially, they would smile and perhaps nod, but over time, they began engaging in brief conversations with me. I realized that for so many years, I had desired to communicate clearly, yet I had held no hope that it would ever happen. I had learned to remain silent, keeping my space around me empty to avoid the disappointed looks and laughter. The only way my teachers knew I possessed a keen intellect was through my test results and the papers I would write. They knew I had a brilliant brain, but they also knew that my words were in constant conflict, vying to be the first to escape.

I chose a Sunday dinner for this significant moment, knowing that my entire family would be present. Sundays were our days to attend church together, and Mother would always prepare a lavish meal. It was a day for our family to stay home and express gratitude for what we had. I waited patiently as my brothers and sisters filled the air with tales of their adventures, as if they were living on a distant island in a different world. I bided my time until Mother shared her week, and

I remembered that my father typically had the fewest words but the most impactful ones. Everyone at the table knew I would either speak last or not at all. However, on this particular Sunday, something felt different. There was an unusual calm in our house, and the attention gradually shifted to me. My father, as he often did, turned to me and asked me to share my week's experiences with the family. Strangely, there was no laughter from my siblings, and there was no disappointment on my mother's face. For some inexplicable reason, I could hear my teacher's voice echoing in my mind, urging me to take my time and allow only one thought to escape at a time.

I opened my mouth, and I spoke three clear sentences without interruption from another thought trying to emerge. On that day, my words aligned perfectly with my thoughts, flowing like a jazz band playing soft notes between sets. My words were akin to a saxophone playing a few smooth notes, evoking a sense of peaceful calm. I spoke those three sentences with confidence and clarity, and then I paused to catch my breath. I remembered my teacher's advice about breathing and composure, and I followed it. As I exhaled and prepared to speak again, I noticed tears running down my mother's almond-colored cheeks. I saw my father leaning back in his chair with his chest proudly puffed out. I also noticed my brothers and sisters were no longer giggling or more interested in dirty dishes than in my words. I was on stage, and my family was now listening to me instead of laughing at me.

That day at the dinner table marked a turning point in my life. It was the day that inspired me to become a writer because I had always expressed myself better on paper than orally. I could gather my thoughts and let them approach my mouth in an orderly manner. But I couldn't help but think back to all the giggles, the disappointed looks, and the ridicule from schoolmates who took pleasure in my struggle.

Recently, a reporter contacted me for an interview about my bestselling book. One of her first questions revolved around my written words and thoughts, and what had inspired me to write in the manner I did. I composed myself, took a deep breath, and allowed my mind to drift back to my childhood. I spoke my father's words: "I simply wanted to fill the empty space in the atmosphere."

Exhausted

Devastated, I couldn't comprehend how he could take such a step. Did he not realize the pending list of tasks I had for him? A list of things that still needed his attention? I glanced once more at the doctor before leaving, hoping his words would somehow change. Maybe he would tell me it was just indigestion or a mistake, that Robert simply needed some medication. I yearned for him to reassure me that it was all a misunderstanding. But deep down, I knew that death was irreversible, that this wasn't some reversible error.

Feeling utterly lost, I stood there, unsure of my next move. My gaze turned to my friend Irma, searching for any sign that she had a different interpretation of the doctor's words. Maybe I was overly stressed, and my hearing had deceived me. I longed for a semblance of normalcy, for someone to tell me that I had misunderstood. As Irma gently took hold of my hand, guiding me towards the exit, her compassionate gesture reminded me of her unwavering support.

"Let's go home. You need to rest," Irma said softly, her voice a soothing balm for my shattered emotions. Her friendship was a constant in my life, a dependable presence even in this heart-wrenching moment. I looked into her eyes, hoping to find solace, only to see a tear glistening. The truth hung heavily in the air. The doctor's declaration of Robert's death wasn't a figment of my imagination or a result of mishearing. It was an agonizing reality that I had to confront. Robert was gone.

Irma took my car keys and drove me home, recognizing that I was in no condition to drive. The world around me felt hazy, and I was grateful for her steadying presence. As I walked through the motions of my daily routine, Irma stepped in to support me. She cleaned the dishes, folded the laundry, and remained by my side, a silent source of comfort during this difficult time.

Grief has a way of playing tricks on your emotions, I realized. It crept up on me unexpectedly, even as I moved mechanically through the tasks that had once felt normal. I found myself in the kitchen, preparing Robert's favorite meal. Red beans and rice simmered on the stove, and a chicken breast roasted in the oven. Irma observed me from her seat in the kitchen, her eyes fixed on me as I followed my routine as if he were still there.

With the beans and rice heated and the chicken cooked to a perfect golden brown, I placed a portion on a plate for Robert and covered it with foil. In my delusion, I announced to Irma that he would enjoy it when he returned home. Looking back, I can see the extent of my denial, how my mind was grasping for any semblance of normalcy. Irma, the kind and understanding friend she is, never confronted my delusions. She never shattered the illusion that Robert was still with us, nor did she point out the painful truth that he wouldn't be coming home again.

In her silent support, Irma provided a buffer between my shattered reality and the harsh truth that I couldn't bring myself to acknowledge. Her presence was a lifeline during those early moments of grief, when the weight of the loss was too much to bear all at once.

That night, after seeing Irma off and closing the side door, I climbed into bed. Sleep evaded me as my mind spun with thoughts of Robert. I tossed and turned, caught in a relentless loop of memories and emotions. At times, I found myself peeking through the curtains, half-expecting to see his truck pulling into the driveway. His voice echoed in my thoughts, each word haunting me with its weight.

Robert's words had a way of resurfacing, replaying in my mind like a broken record. He would often jest that I was working him to his death. Thirty years of labor on his job, and even in retirement, I'd never let up with my lists of tasks. Yard work, repairs, odd jobs – there was always something waiting for him. Robert wasn't keen on mowing the lawn; he believed his long work hours justified hiring local boys to do it. In my eyes, this refusal signaled laziness, a trait I was determined not to tolerate, regardless of age.

When he retired, my plan was set in motion. Before he could even settle into his recliner, my agenda of daily chores was ready. The shutters needed a fresh coat of paint, the dryer demanded attention, and leaves clogged the gutters thanks to our towering magnolia tree. The list went on, and Robert's resistance grew.

He pushed back, asserting his desire for relaxation. He reminded me of the years he'd spent toiling at the warehouse, the weekends he sacrificed moving furniture and hauling loads to make extra money. He accused me of being a dictator, incredulous that I, someone who had never held a formal job, would dare to dictate his actions. His frustration was palpable, his argument highlighting his own sacrifices and my lack of outside employment.

It was true, my upbringing had instilled in me traditional gender roles – that women belonged in the kitchen and the bedroom. I had never ventured into the world of paid employment, yet I prided myself on maintaining a tidy home and ensuring Robert had a warm meal awaiting him after his workday.

Amid his heated outburst, Robert's anger eventually subsided, and he returned to his recliner. For a span of about two weeks, he found solace in television, until one day he reached for the list of tasks I had set out. His demeanor had changed; he seemed resigned to the idea that he might as well tackle some work. He commented that enduring the company of a disgruntled woman was driving him up the wall. To me, it wasn't mere complaining but a desire to see a man engaged rather than idling around the house. Our financial needs were met, with Robert's pension and army benefits more than sufficient. My perspective centered on motivating him, urging him to be active, as my upbringing had taught me that a man's duty wasn't to be idle.

My father had been a hard worker until his very last day, a role model of diligence. I held Robert to a similar standard, and we frequently debated the hours he spent reclining in seeming inactivity. These thoughts and memories now revisit me as I lay in bed, struggling to sleep. They resurface like shadows, causing me to question if I played a role in Robert's passing. Was my insistence on keeping him active too much? Should I have allowed him days of restful leisure? The idea of a grown man sinking into slumber in his chair during the day weighed heavily on me. It seemed a sign of indolence, an attitude I couldn't accept.

I wrestle with these memories, trying to quiet the echoes of our arguments. Robert's words linger in my mind – how he often claimed I would work him into his grave. The weight of guilt looms large as I wonder if I inadvertently pushed him too hard, if my insistence on activity contributed to his demise. The fear that my actions might have truly worked him to his death consumes me.

On the day Robert passed away, he was up on the roof, replacing worn-out tiles. Though he preferred to have his friend Carl from a roofing company handle the task, I insisted that he was capable of doing it himself. That morning, I handed Robert my list of tasks as usual, adding a note at the bottom specifically about the roof tiles that had been neglected for weeks. My urgency was fueled by my desire to prevent squirrels from infiltrating our attic. Despite the oppressive humidity of a typical New Orleans summer, I believed that with focused effort, he could finish the job swiftly.

Robert positioned his painter's ladder right by the kitchen window, affording me a clear view of his progress. As he ascended, he grumbled incessantly. Even as he passed by the window, he took a moment to complain about how I was going to be the end of him one day. He jokingly claimed that I'd be responsible for his funeral, insisting that I only seemed content when I saw him working hard and sweating. His words stung, but I simply waved him off with my dish towel, not in the mood to engage in a conversation filled with complaints. All I cared about was getting those roof tiles fixed to safeguard my attic.

So when I turned back to the window and called out to Robert, it wasn't to exchange more complaints. I admonished him about being lazy, reiterating my unwavering stance on laziness regardless of age. Just then, my attention shifted. I noticed Jeffery Miller, a neighborhood kid, rushing toward our house. Jeffery had taken over the lawn-mowing duties that Robert used to handle. Robert had handed him a twenty-dollar bill every week in exchange for his services, a task that I had previously insisted Robert do. I withheld water from Jeffery while he worked, refusing to aid in diminishing Robert's responsibilities. Confused about why Jeffery was racing to our house, I wondered what might have prompted this unexpected visit, especially considering my reluctance to let him mow our lawn.

As I pulled back the curtains to see why Jeffery was rushing towards our house, I noticed a look of panic etched on his face. However, what truly alarmed me was the expression on our neighbor Mrs. Rita's face, accompanied by her husband Melvin's even more distressed appearance. Rita pointed urgently towards the ground, causing me to look down and see Robert lying there, completely still. A mixture of confusion and annoyance washed over me – how could he be so indolent as to lie on the ground in front of our neighbors? But in a heartbeat, my thoughts shifted as I saw more neighbors rushing towards him. Could he actually be hurt? It was a concept that I initially couldn't fathom.

Rita called for an ambulance, and Irma arrived at my side door, ready to assist me. We stood there, both of us hovering over Robert, searching for any sign of life, any indication that he was okay, but there was no movement, no response. The paramedics arrived, placing him on a gurney and fitting an oxygen mask over his nose. Despite their efforts, there was no sign of breath escaping from his mouth.

I got into my car, Irma by my side, and followed the ambulance to the hospital. There, I received news that no wife ever wants to hear

— news that no woman wants to hear about her husband. The words echoed in my ears, delivering the painful truth that Robert was gone.

Just as before, Irma reached out and guided me, this time back home. "Let's get you home, you need to get some rest," she said, her compassion unwavering. Irma had always been a dependable friend, a source of comfort. Now, my days are filled with the torment of wondering if I pushed Robert to his death through my insistence on work. Nightmares haunt my sleep, and his voice echoes in my mind, a constant reminder of the arguments we had.

If only I had let him be, let him enjoy his retirement without pushing him into constant activity. Now, faced with this void, I wonder who would want a sixty-seven-year-old woman. Who will be there for me, and who will I care for in return? The weight of regret and guilt looms heavy, leaving me with questions and a profound sense of loss. Most importantly, who will fulfill my list of duties around the house.

Past Life

Six o'clock in the morning, another workday begins. My days usually start early and ends late, but I don't mind. I rise, kiss my wife, and pass by my two kids' rooms. Planting kisses on their foreheads, I then proceed to the shower. Before leaving for work, my wife has already prepared coffee and toast for my drive. I manage a national chain retail store, not just a neighborhood mom-and-pop shop. This chain boasts over six thousand locations across the United States. Reflecting on where I started in life, I feel incredibly fortunate to be working for this company and to have a family. Sometimes, the emotions associated with this overwhelm me.

One day, while waiting at a red light, the weight of it all hit me, and I couldn't control my emotions. Tears streamed down my face as I wailed there at the red light, bewildering the people in the adjacent car.

I was once advised not to worry about tomorrow, as today has enough problems of its own. Little did I know that today would present the challenge I hoped would never materialize. Today is our company's job fair, held at the location I manage. It's an honor that my manager and the company have such confidence in me to host this event. As I approach the parking lot, I see a crowd of people eagerly waiting for us to open so they can fill out applications. This situation resembles a lottery, given our infrequent mass hiring sessions. Our staff tends to be loyal, and it's the kind of job people usually don't leave. Some employees have been with the company even longer than I have, attracted by our competitive wages and consistent top-five ranking in terms of employee benefits and bonuses.

As I unlock the store to allow my employees inside and reassure the eager crowd that we'll be opening on time for the scheduled job fair, I notice two men gazing at me. Their persistent arm-waving suggests they recognize me, but I can't place them. Despite the curiosity, I shrug it off and proceed to open the store. My focus is on ensuring everything is ready for the impending visit from my manager and the corporate executives. This event could be a significant opportunity for my family and me.

The job fair's success and the executives' impression of me could be the catalyst for a much-awaited promotion. A move up the ladder to Division Manager would mean increased earnings, stock options, and a company car. The stakes are high, and I'm meticulous about every detail to ensure a flawless execution.

As my manager approaches, he greets me with a handshake and a quiet word. He emphasizes that this could be the moment for my advancement. He, too, has his eyes on a promotion, aiming for the role of Regional Vice President. Our aspirations are intertwined in this job fair, and we're both dedicated to its success. While my performance metrics suggest I'm ready for the next level, the corporate executives want to gauge my interpersonal skills and how I interact with both my team and customers.

Their arrival brings reassurance, as they assure me that things will go well and that this visit is largely a formality. I take a deep breath, pause to glance at a photo of my wife and kids in my wallet, and offer a quick prayer. This day has been a long time coming, ever since I entered the business a few years ago. My determination is unwavering – I'm driven to make this visit and job fair as flawless as possible.

As the morning unfolds and the influx of applicants fills the store, I again notice the two men waving at me. Despite their familiarity, I remain perplexed, and I continue with my routine of managing the store's operations, ensuring shelves are stocked, and promotions are properly marked. Amid this, the store's loudspeaker calls for a manager to answer the phone. My heart flutters, anticipating a call from my wife wishing me well. Her warm voice indeed greets me, filling me with confidence and pride. In this moment, nothing seems capable of tainting this pinnacle in my career.

As I finish the call, one of my colleagues approaches and informs me that two men are seeking me out at the front register. Apparently, they're from the job fair and have asked for me using a rather peculiar name – something along the lines of "DooDirty." I feel a rush of embarrassment, fearing that my past is catching up with me at the worst possible time.

Despite my nervousness, I instruct my colleague to return to her post and assure her that I'll handle the situation. Gathering my composure, I approach the register with a welcoming smile and extend my hand to greet the two men. Before I can even ask how I can assist them, they burst into laughter. One of them engulfs me in a bear hug, leaving me taken aback.

With joviality, they remind me of their earlier waving antics during the store's opening. My heart sinks as they inquire if I'm the "world-famous Don DooDirty." I sense that they recognize me from a past life, a life I had hoped to leave behind. Trying to distance myself from that identity, I suggest we step outside for a private conversation away from the prying eyes of corporate personnel. I'm acutely aware that I cannot let anyone with influence over my promotion see me engaged with these men.

As we reach the parking lot, they persist with their questioning, repeating their inquiry about the "world-famous Don DooDirty." I maintain a professional demeanor, denying any association with that name. However, they erupt in laughter once again, showering me with hugs and shouting "Triple D in the house." Despite my attempts to convince them otherwise, their familiarity suggests they see through my façade.

Deep down, I acknowledge their accurate recognition, but I continue to deny it outwardly. Inwardly conflicted, I grapple with the collision of my past and present, the weight of my ambition, and the unexpected reappearance of a part of my life I had long tried to put behind me.

I inquire if there's anything specific they need assistance with, while conveying my need to return to work if not. Their laughter fills the air as they apologize, acknowledging their awareness of my situation and promising not to expose my secret. Beneath my external calm, a sense of relief washes over me. These two men had a front-row seat to my past life, holding knowledge about me that I've intentionally buried.

With a light-hearted tone, they admit their admiration for my "game" and assure me they won't reveal my true identity. My gratitude for their discretion is mingled with a hint of nostalgia, knowing that their presence harkens back to a chapter of my life I've striven to move beyond.

They broach the topic of employment, sharing their desire for a steady nine-to-five job. The allure of their past days in the hip-hop scene has waned, replaced by a practical need to provide for their families and establish stability. Their aspirations align with securing a position that offers financial support and a reliable routine.

These men, while not the prominent artists or producers, were integral behind-the-scenes figures, handling the less glamorous aspects of the industry. They were connected, whether it was sourcing drugs, arranging encounters, acquiring jewelry, or procuring funds. The juxtaposition of their past roles against my current life is a stark reminder of the distance I've traveled, leaving behind a world that no longer resonates with who I've become.

While I continue to outwardly suppress my past, the meeting with these men unearths memories and emotions that challenge the facade I've built. As they articulate their desire for stability, I find myself reflecting on the transformation my life has undergone, the opportunities that have come my way, and the family that now anchors me.

With an outwardly friendly demeanor, I assure them that I'll personally handle their applications and move to wrap up our conversation, hoping they'll move along. However, internally, my intentions are quite different. My plan is to retrieve their applications, not for the purpose of processing them, but to ensure they're thoroughly destroyed in my shredder. The last thing I need is a piece of my past infiltrating my present life. My past is something I've worked hard to distance myself from, and I'm resolute in maintaining that separation.

My transformation has been deliberate. I've gone to great lengths to shed the markers of my past identity. The tattoos are gone, the gold teeth replaced with more conventional dental work. The goatee, once a signature, is now clean-shaven, and my hairstyle has been updated. I've traded in the baggy jeans and flashy boots for slacks and penny loafers. The flashy jewelry is gone; now, my only adornment is a wedding ring. This change has been a deliberate effort to redefine myself. Hip-hop, which once consumed my identity, now feels like a distant chapter, a phase that no longer defines me.

I've transformed from Don DooDirty into Donald Morgan, the manager of a major retail store. The rap world was a chapter of my life that I've closed. I once immersed myself in Black hip-hop culture, embracing its mannerisms, style, and even relationships. At that time, I felt like an outsider seeking acceptance. My passion for music and business drew me into a world where talent transcended racial boundaries, but it was also a world where I felt I needed to adopt a new persona to belong.

Now, I stand as a changed man. I've learned that identity is complex and can't be confined to external markers. I've matured and evolved beyond that phase, recognizing the value of authenticity over conformity. My White skin is no longer a canvas for projecting a persona. I've embraced my own identity, my own path, and my own values. As for the two men from my past, their situations highlight the complexities they face, particularly given their racial identities. While I've successfully reinvented myself, they remain grounded in their identity as Black men, an aspect they can't alter.

The encounter with these men serves as a reminder of the journey I've undertaken, the bridges I've burned, and the transformative power of personal growth.

In my case, being White on the outside has allowed me to better conceal my past and strive for a new future. I don't possess any superior education or intelligence compared to these men, but what sets me apart is my ability to blend into any crowd, maintaining the façade of a changed man. Removing my tattoos, replacing my gold teeth caps, altering my appearance, and refining my speech and mannerisms have contributed to the transformation. Opting for a fresh start, I moved away from my hometown to a remote location, distancing myself from the persona of Don DooDirty. I used a portion of my earnings to purchase a modest home and transitioned to a more inconspicuous lifestyle.

An associate's degree from a local community college introduced me to my now-wife, who knows nothing of my previous life in the rap industry. This aspect of my life remains hidden, a secret I'm determined to preserve. Curiosity gnaws at me regarding how these two men found themselves in the same small town, which houses only a handful of Black residents. I surmise that they, too, sought anonymity and chose a location where they could escape notice.

My manager's appearance in the parking lot snaps me back to the present. I reassure him that I was simply assisting the two men with inquiries about the job fair. I'm aware of the urgency to return to the store; the executives' presence demands my attention. I reassure the two men that I am not Don DooDirty and pledge to explore employment options for them. While outwardly promising, my intent is to ensure their applications are permanently disposed of. I can't risk anyone from my past crossing paths with my current life – a life I've painstakingly constructed to distance myself from that persona.

Returning to the store, I reassure my manager that there's no connection between me and the men. As the job fair concludes and the day progresses, I can't shake thoughts of those two men who knew the truth about me. Reflecting on my history, I acknowledge that while I took advantage of the rap industry's dynamics, my exit was always a planned step. The culture didn't define me; I integrated myself into it for personal gain.

My hopes extend to those two men, although I wish them well outside the realm of my store. My success hinges on shielding my former life from exposure. My family's stability and my aspirations for a better future drive my actions. I remain so removed from the rap culture that I've forsaken it even from my personal playlist.

As I arrive home in my quiet subdivision, thoughts churn about whether I should confess to my wife. The fear of her reaction weighs heavy – will she still love me, or will our marriage crumble? Amid these concerns, I contemplate the fate of the men who unearthed my past. Parking the SUV, I enter a house filled with the comfort of home – the aroma of pot roast, the sound of kids playing, and the news on TV. These simple moments reinforce my resolve to safeguard my new life and all that it holds.

The Try Out

In my first week at my new high school, my primary focus wasn't on meeting new teachers or making new friends. Instead, all my attention was directed towards making the basketball team. For the past three years, I had been one of the top players in the Catholic league. However, this new high school didn't participate in the Catholic league basketball. It was a public school, and things would be different.

On top of that, I knew there would be new faces on the court, and I would be playing against guys who were two or three years older than me – players who had the experience of competing in high school basketball, while I had been dominating in the Catholic school league.

The first practice was scheduled for 7 o'clock on the following Monday morning. My mind wasn't preoccupied with my new homeroom teacher or learning the names of my new classmates. My sole concern revolved around signing up for the tryouts and ensuring that I was in the gym on Monday morning before anyone else.

I don't recall much about the weekend; it passed in a blur. My mother's inquiries about my new school and teachers went unanswered as I spent those days obsessively spinning the ball on my fingertips. Practicing moves and refining my ball-handling skills consumed my every waking moment, to the extent that I even skipped church on Sunday.

When Monday morning arrived, I was up and out of the house by 6 o'clock. I brushed past my mother's attempts to offer me breakfast, too focused on my goal to stop and eat.

"Son, you need to eat. You can't expect to be at your best if your stomach is empty. It won't take more than a few minutes to have breakfast. Sit down, and I will ask your daddy to drive you to school, but you need to eat."

Her words fell on deaf ears as I hurried past her towards the front door. "Bye, ma. I'll be back this evening, and hopefully, I'll have good news. Bye!"

Arriving at school promptly at 6:45 am, I made a beeline for the gymnasium. To my surprise, I wasn't the only one who had the idea of arriving early. There were already kids playing on the court, and others were stretching beside the folded bleachers.

As I entered the gym, I was greeted by an emphatic voice booming, "Son, are you on the sign-up list to try out today? If your name isn't on the list, there's no need for you to be here." It was the assistant coach for the junior varsity, the one person whose approval I needed to secure, along with that of the head coach.

"I signed up last week," I replied, my voice slightly shaky. Glancing at his clipboard, I spotted my name towards the bottom of the sign-up sheet. Nervously pointing it out, I added, "There's my name, right there, sir, towards the bottom of the page."

The assistant coach checked off my name and instructed me to spend a few minutes stretching before the tryouts began. Making my way to the bleachers, I started stretching when a loud whistle pierced the air, and the coach yelled, "Junior varsity tryouts on this side of the floor and Varsity tryouts on the other side. Let's go, let's get moving, I don't have all day."

Joining the line with other freshmen and sophomores at one end of the court, we prepared for layup drills. The coach called out, "Right-hand layups first, and then we'll switch to left-hand layups. Boys, if you can't lay the ball up with either hand, then today will be your last day of practice. I will ask you to leave my gym."

This assignment felt like a piece of cake to me, easy and sweet. I had mastered those skills years ago. Shooting about ten layups, five with each hand, I made all of them with ease. Some of the other guys missed their layups, and a few could only shoot with one hand. The assistant coach summoned those guys over to the sidelines, and with dejected looks on their faces, they exited the gym and headed toward the locker room.

Trying to maintain my focus on the court, it was disheartening to witness those guys' dreams of making the team come to an abrupt end.

Once again, the sound of the whistle pierced the air, and the coach's voice echoed, "With the guys I have left on the court, I want you to break off into teams of two. Let's see how you handle pick and roll situations—layups only. If you shoot from the outside, you might as well pack your bags and join the others who were asked to leave."

The assistant coach pointed at me and said, "Pair up with Jackson over there. He'll be your teammate. You two will go against Moore and Elwood. Pick and roll only, layups only." Glancing over, I saw Moore and Elwood, clad in official school practice shorts and shirts, indicating their previous year's team membership. An air of arrogance surrounded them, signaling their experience from last year's squad.

Walking onto the court, Jackson looked at me and said, "Hey, kid, no matter what, just run the pick and roll like the coach said. This is my chance and yours to make the team. Don't mess it up by being a showoff. I noticed you were hitting shots in the layup line. Keep it simple and effective."

We stepped onto the court, and the whistle blew to start the pick and roll drill. Initially, nerves had my legs trembling, but I quickly settled in. Jackson and I performed decently. While Moore and Elwood outperformed us due to their experience, Jackson and I also had moments of success.

After twenty minutes and observing other kids run the drill, the coach blew the whistle again and called out, "Okay, I've seen enough. Everyone, head to the showers and get ready for your first-period class. I'll speak to each of you individually and let you know if you're coming back tomorrow. I appreciate everyone who tried out today and wish you all good luck in the future."

I started packing my bag and getting ready to head to the downstairs showers when Jackson approached me and said, "Hey, not bad. At least you didn't mess it up."

I extended my hand for a fist bump, but Jackson turned away and said, "Let's hold off on the handshake until we find out if we made the team. I only fist bump teammates, not guys who aren't ballplayers."

Just as I was about to reply to Jackson, a hand landed on my shoulder. It was the assistant coach. "Kid, I like how you handled yourself today. Good ball-handling skills and awareness. I also appreciate your response when Moore and Elwood got physical with you. Be here tomorrow, on time and ready to show me more. I want you on my team, but you'll have to prove yourself every day, and I'll expect to see improvement."

I thanked the coach and rushed downstairs, passing the locker room. I was so excited that I forgot I was still wearing gym shorts and a t-shirt. The need for a shower and making it to my first-period class slipped my mind. Admittedly, my focus wasn't on school that day. Later, as I headed to my fourth-period class, I saw Jackson in the hallway. He was conversing with a few of the other guys I recognized from the tryouts. Jackson said, "Guys, let me talk to this kid for a moment. I'll be right back."

Jackson moved past one of the guys as if executing a screen play. "Hey, kid, I just saw the list posted outside the coach's office. You made the Junior Varsity team, and so did I. Looks like we'll be teammates now." With those words, Jackson extended his hand with a look of connection on his face, and we exchanged a fist bump.

One Last Chance

Life hadn't always been easy for me, especially during my upbringing. Both my parents were present in our household, but one of them had an insatiable lust for the streets. It was as if there was an irresistible call from the outside world that beckoned him each evening.

He followed the same routine with a religious devotion. After returning from work, he would lovingly kiss my mother on the cheek, ruffle my hair, and exclaim, "Hey there, my boy!" as he began to shed his work shirt. We would all gather around the table for our meal, with my mother ensuring that he was served first. Casting a stern gaze at me, she would say, "Remember, I've spoken to you about sneaking into the pots. Your daddy works tirelessly, and any man who puts in such hard work deserves the first bite. Sit down, be patient. Your daddy isn't a selfish man, and he always leaves plenty for the two of us."

True to her words, my father wasn't selfish at all, ensuring there was always enough for both my mother and me. Dinner times became special because it was one of the rare periods when my father was consistently present. When he wasn't rushing off to work, he was heading to the pool hall, the race track, or the barroom. He believed that a man who toiled to provide a home and sustenance for his family deserved to relish life's pleasures. He found joy in a good game of pool, the excitement of watching horses race, and the company of charming women over a drink.

Nothing could deter him from his pursuits. He was unwavering in his determination to extract every ounce of experience life had to offer. These are the memories I hold dear from my childhood. There wasn't a chance for him to teach me how to play sports; I picked up those skills by spending time at the park or engaging in neighborhood games with my friends. A twinge of envy would sometimes surface as I watched my buddies toss the football around with their fathers. I longed for my father to do the same with me, but I understood that he needed to work, and his leisure time followed his work.

I carried this situation from my young life into adulthood, and as a grown man, I made a solemn promise to myself that if I ever had a son, I would prioritize spending meaningful time with him. I had grown to understand the value of not rushing into marriage and was determined not to bring children into the world unless I was married.

Embracing the single life, I appreciated the freedom that came with it, knowing that my choices and movements wouldn't impact a wife or child.

But then, life took an unexpected turn. I was browsing the aisles of the grocery store when I heard my phone's ringer go off. Glancing at the screen, I noticed several missed calls. I answered, and the voice on the other end was nearly unrecognizable. I inquired, offering help to the distressed person on the line. Amidst sobbing and muffled words, I realized it was my father.

"Son, do you have a moment?" Without waiting for my response, he launched into the reason for his distress. "I just got back from the doctor's office, and she delivered some tough news. Its cancer, and it's advanced. I don't know what steps to take, my boy. If your mother were here, she'd know what to do, but she's gone. I've never felt this lost in my life. I can't even remember where I parked my car. I'm completely adrift, son, please help me."

In moments like these, an unpleasant side of us can emerge – the side that recalls all those evenings that could have been spent together but weren't. It's the side that resents the choice to play pool instead of teaching me how to throw a football, the allure of the horse race commentator's voice over quality time, and the instances of seeking companionship in a barroom rather than listening to my early attempts at reading aloud.

That vengeful aspect looms, I won't deny it. The thoughts of finally letting him know how I felt have raced through my mind countless times. However, this wasn't the moment for that. Given his condition, I questioned whether such an opportunity would ever present itself.

There were more pressing matters at hand than venting my anger and frustration about his life choices. I had carved out a respectable path for myself and achieved self-sufficiency. It's not as if he left me in poverty and despair; he instilled many qualities in me. My mother, too, contributed qualities – compassion and kindness being amongst them.

Taking a moment to steady my thoughts, I absorbed the weight of my father's words. With a sigh, I found my voice and said, "My mother would know what to do. Let's find a silver lining in this dark news. Pack your things and let your landlord know you're moving out. Come live with me; let me take care of you. Don't reject my offer. We're family, and in times like this, I believe it's my responsibility to look after you."

On the other end of the line, the sound of sobbing filled the air. Amid the tears, my father managed to say, "Son, I'll do whatever you ask. I never saw this coming. I was prepared to face this alone at home. You're just like your mother."

I cared for my father diligently until the day they laid him to rest. Countless nights, I would help him with his shower, trim his hair, or provide a close shave. It wasn't merely a sense of duty that drove me, but a deep-rooted love. During those long, quiet hours, we would converse until the early morning. Through those conversations, I gleaned insights about him that had eluded me before. I uncovered the intricacies of his character and the reasons that compelled him to wander the streets so frequently. He explained that it was how his father lived life. It was his example and he followed it to the last letter.

I began this journey with the intention of giving him one last opportunity, a chance to make amends for not being there during the times I yearned for his presence. Yet, that last chance seemed to be as much for me as it was for him. Through our shared moments, I unearthed the details of his life and gained a closeness that both of us desperately needed. These instances granted me a fresh perspective and provided the means to heal the wounds from my youthful days.

In the end, those moments we spent together allowed me to take a step forward, freeing myself from the pain of my earlier years. The past's hurt was gradually replaced with the understanding and connection that had previously been absent.

Upside Down

I am no longer just a visitor; I have become a citizen of New Orleans. I relocated to the city on a temporary basis right after Hurricane Katrina as part of a medical team. Our mission was to provide basic healthcare to the citizens who had endured the storm's wrath. I wasn't entirely sure what to anticipate. Like many who had never been to the city, I had a preconceived notion that it would solely revolve around Bourbon Street. I held visions of exotic cocktails and nightclubs that never closed.

To my surprise, Bourbon Street was indeed still vibrant and active even in the aftermath of such a catastrophic event. However, despite living here for five years, I never found myself venturing to Bourbon Street.

I chose to establish my home here due to the resilience and character of the people I was assisting. The residents of New Orleans are predominantly humble, kind, and often exceedingly polite. Such gestures were unfamiliar to me, having spent my entire life in Texas where people could at times be reserved and many surly. While they would step forward in times of necessity, otherwise, they often maintained their distance. In New Orleans, I was struck by the everyday acts of kindness. Despite enduring a devastating storm that not only robbed them of their belongings but also claimed lives, the people remained cheerful and appreciative.

My initial profound encounter with this spirit occurred after a particularly demanding day. We had a distressed mother visit our office seeking assistance for her asthmatic daughter. She arrived right as we were closing for the day, and the entire staff, myself included, were thoroughly exhausted. Having endured a grueling twelve-hour shift, we were eager to lock up and head home. The woman, however, persisted in seeking help for her daughter. Reluctantly, I opened the door, hoping that no one else would follow.

In a hurry, the woman entered with her daughter tightly clinging to her side. It was evident that the young girl was struggling to breathe. Swiftly, we administered a breathing treatment, and the doctor promptly began drafting a prescription for her required medication.

Exhaustion had taken its toll on me, pushing me to the brink of my patience. I yearned for a cigarette break and one of those famous daiquiris. Once the young girl's condition had stabilized and she could breathe without struggle, we discharged her. Her mother's parting words were a stern, frustrated "Thank you."

As I followed her towards the door to unlock it, the mother turned, her eyes glistening with tears, and spoke softly, "I apologize for my attitude. This whole aftermath situation is incredibly tough. It weighs on my daughter and myself. I'm just a worried mother and a person grappling with frustration. Your efforts shouldn't be the target, so please don't take it personally."

With those words, she extended her arms, offering a heartfelt embrace. Her hug was anything but ordinary. It carried within it genuine feelings of love, care, and pain all intertwined. As she walked to her car, her daughter looked back and waved a final goodbye.

Weary and drained, I headed to my desk to retrieve my timecard for clocking out. My colleague greeted me with a smile, remarking, "Welcome to New Orleans—the city where someone might reprimand you one moment and embrace you the next."

We chuckled, sharing a cigarette in the parking lot. Our conversation flowed for the next hour. The laughter had a transformative effect on my soul that no daiquiris could replicate. I felt rejuvenated and inspired regarding my job and my place in this world. For the first time in a long while, I experienced a sense of belonging and significance.

After a year filled with bowls of gumbo, heaps of seafood, and vibrant interactions, the time came for me to consider returning to Texas. However, a persistent feeling within my soul refused to let me leave. I concocted every conceivable excuse to prolong my stay in New Orleans. I convinced myself that the patients depended solely on me, that no other medical personnel could provide the same level of care. I extended my stay for another month to witness Mardi gras, then another month for another festival, followed by football and basketball seasons.

Amidst this cycle of excuses, I found myself remaining for an additional year. I recall making calls back home to check on my parents, only to learn from my mother that my former boyfriend had been reaching out. He was never a serious suitor—just someone pleasant to spend time with and share a drink or two. I recognized that our fling couldn't evolve into anything substantial.

Gradually, it dawned on me that I had suspended my life for two years, and the desire to return to Texas had dwindled. I used to proclaim that regardless of where life took me, I would always be a Texan at heart. Yet, my perspective had evolved. I now regarded myself as a true citizen of New Orleans. While I hadn't been born there, I felt an undeniable connection to the city and its inhabitants.

You might be inclined to think that merely residing in a city for a brief period couldn't alter one's fundamental essence, but I respectfully disagree. This city exudes vitality, and its people embody that vibrancy. A shared passion for food, music, and humanity thrives here. I've fallen in love, though not with my former beau. Instead, it's this city and its people that have captured my heart. The world I once knew has been turned upside down, and curiously, it's a profoundly positive sensation.

King of the Park

It was the summer of 1980, and it also marked my high school years as both a student and an athlete. It was that phase of life when you're at the pinnacle of your athletic prowess, and confidence seems to overflow. I believe it was a combination of my skill level on the court and the attention I received from the girls in the neighborhood. The girls would say my name slowly, with a certain drawl, and wave at me with intentions that my parents had warned me about.

My mother, in particular, would often preach, "Boy, don't go out there and catch something, or worse, bring a child into this world at sixteen years old." I would usually laugh it off, but my mother's concern was genuine. My father, too, was deeply concerned. He had been an athlete himself, and he and my mother had started dating in high school. He was more cautious about the girls who hung around our block and which college coaches I was able to talk to. He had walked down a similar path and was well-acquainted with the pitfalls that awaited me. My father wanted nothing but the best for me, and he wanted me out of New Orleans and on to college as soon as possible.

His words still echo in my mind like a broken record on rewind. "Son, I've seen this city consume so many gifted ballplayers, and I don't want your name to be on the list of those who could have achieved greatness but didn't. Leave those girls alone, focus on honing your skills, and keep your grades up. Remember, son, it's both your grades and your game that will pave the way out of here."

I obediently followed my father's advice and was attentive to my mother's wishes. I wasn't foolish, and I was well aware that I had a promising future ahead. I didn't harbor any naive dreams of going professional, but I knew that basketball could pave the way for my college education. I had played against some of the local college players, and many of them had told me that I had the potential to play at the college level. This filled me with excitement, and I was eager to choose a college.

As for now, it was the summer, the last summer of my high school years. My friends and I had a daily routine of heading to the playground. Some of us would walk there, while others rode their bicycles alongside us. During these walks, we talked about our dreams and what life had in store for us. Most of the guys were quite talkative, and some wouldn't stop until they had exhausted their words. In contrast, I tended to keep quiet and to myself. Occasionally, I'd stop and exchange greetings with people sitting on their porches, individuals who were familiar with my parents. Other times, I'd pause and engage in a brief conversation with a girl who was a fervent enthusiast of our basketball games.

This one particular girl always stood at the corner of New Orleans Street and Law Street, right before we entered the park. She was insistent on getting close to me and whispering in my ear. As my mother would say, she was a fast girl—too mature for her age, and certainly too fast for my liking. She seemed like a trap, and I was well aware of the dangers of getting caught in such a snare.

My friends and I would enter the park around three thirty, just as the scorching heat was starting to relent a bit. We approached the park with an air of confidence, as if we were entering a professional arena. Everyone in the neighborhood knew us, and they eagerly anticipated our arrival because they understood that once we took the court, victory was almost assured. The five of us strolled onto the court with our heads held high, exuding confidence from every pore. Typically, I would be the one to shout out, "We got next!" It was as if we were announcing that any hopes or dreams of defeating us should be set aside. We were here, and we had no intentions of leaving until the sun began its descent.

We'd dominate the court for hours on end, but we always remained vigilant, keeping an eye on our surroundings and the time. We didn't need a watch to gauge the time; we could tell by the way the sun started to dip behind the row of shotgun houses in the neighborhood. We always knew when it was time to leave—except for that one fateful day. On that occasion, we were playing exceptionally well, and the neighborhood had turned out in force to watch us in action. We played our hearts out but lost track of time and our surroundings.

As the sun made its final appearance, the park lights started to flicker on. Normally, we would have been long gone before the park lights illuminated, but today, our overconfidence had kept us lingering. We were just about to wrap up the game, desperately trying to reach twenty-one to end it, when our worst fear materialized. The other "king of the court" arrived, a guy named Al. Al and I had attended elementary school together, and he had some basketball skills. While he wasn't on the elite level of myself and my friends, he could definitely hold his own. Al had dropped out of school and opted for a life on the streets. Initially, he was known as a hustler who stole bikes or broke into cars. However, he had since graduated to dealing drugs, and he had a notorious reputation in the neighborhood. He often used the playground basketball court as his makeshift office.

I urgently yelled to one of my friends, "Come on, man, hit the shot so we can go!" As the ball swished through the net, bringing the game to an end, we hurried to collect our bags from the side of the court. I made brief eye contact with Al and gave him a slight nod, saying, "What's up, Al?"

Al had a certain look about him that exuded confidence, but his confidence was of a different kind than mine. My confidence stemmed from being a superior basketball player compared to most guys in the neighborhood. Al's confidence, on the other hand, was rooted in the fact that he knew people were afraid of him. There was an aura around him that screamed danger, and it was clear that he wouldn't hesitate to resort to violence at the drop of a dime.

As we passed each other, Al called out, "Playboy, why are you in such a rush? No need to hurry home just yet. Remember back in elementary school when we used to play on the blacktop, and I was on your team from time to time? You were always head and shoulders above the other kids. I used to hope we'd be on opposite teams just so I could challenge you. I wanted to prove that I was better, but it never happened. You were so much better than everyone else. That was then, but this is now, and I know I'm a better shooter than you if I put my mind to it."

I tried to downplay Al's words with a slight laugh and a quick response, saying, "Yeah, I remember those days; you were pretty good." I kept the conversation brief as my friends and I gathered our gym bags and began making our way toward the gate to leave. However, before we could exit, Al called out again, "Why are you rushing, playboy? Why not stick around and see if we can settle this with a shooting contest, just you and me? Your buddies can watch. One shot from the top of the key, fifty dollars on the line."

I turned to look at my friends, attempting to hide my reluctance, but at the same time, I couldn't back down from a challenge. Once you reach a certain level of skill and confidence, there's no room for backing down from any challenge, no matter how unexpected. Furthermore, my friends had a particular image of me that I couldn't afford to damage. With a nervous chuckle, I replied to Al, "Al, you know I don't have that kind of cash on me right now. All I've got is enough for a snowball on my way home. Maybe we can do this when I start making real money like you."

Al didn't seem swayed by my initial response. He swiftly snatched my basketball from under my arms and declared, "Come on, playboy. I know you don't carry cash like I do, but we can still settle this with a shot from the top of the key. If you win, I'll let you and your friends come back here tomorrow. If you lose, I don't want to see you cocky kids in this park ever again. Even if I hear that you set foot in this park, there will be trouble for you. I'm not giving you a choice here. Put your bag down and come out onto the court. This won't take long—just one shot. If we both make it, then we'll keep shooting until one of us misses."

I reluctantly set my bag down and started walking back onto the court. One of my friends chimed in, saying, "Come on, man, this is easy work. Make the shot, and let's get out of here!" I turned toward him with an irritated look on my face and snapped, "Man, shut up! This isn't a game for him."

I made my way to the top of the key where Al was waiting with my basketball in his hand. He was trying to spin the ball on his finger, but it kept slipping. I knew better than to comment on it. Normally, if someone tried to be cocky with me, I'd have a quick retort ready. But Al was different. He wasn't a ballplayer; he was a dealer. While a ballplayer might let a bit of trash talk slide, a guy like Al might use it as an excuse for violence.

I turned to look at my friends, hoping for a boost of confidence, but they seemed a bit shaken too. The girls from the neighborhood had gathered by the chain-link fence, chatting amongst themselves. I realized I needed to maintain my confidence while keeping my cool. Al dribbled the ball, and it was clear that he hadn't dribbled in a while. The ball was bouncing off his leg, and he was having trouble maintaining a grip on it. He declared, "Just one shot, playboy. That's all I need to make it."

Al leaned back and launched a shot toward the basket. The ball hit the metal backboard with a resounding clang and was nowhere near the mark. He missed the shot, and it wasn't even close. Al turned to me, his expression bearing an intensity that few had witnessed, and he said, "Okay, I missed. You better make it. If you miss, I don't want to see you or your friends in this park ever again. Now go ahead and take your shot, playboy."

A top-of-the-key shot was a breeze for me. I could make it with my eyes closed, and I had the ability to shoot it with either hand. I took a few dribbles and started to contemplate my options. Should I make the shot and assert my superiority, or should I intentionally miss to satisfy his ego? I avoided looking at my friends or the girls gathered by the fence. Finally, I stopped dribbling and took the shot. It swished through the net without touching the rim. My friends started to cheer, but I shot them a look that silently said, "Guys, keep it down."

Al looked at me and said, "Playboy, you were always the better shooter, but don't let that get to your head. I usually come out on top in everything I do, so don't let me catch wind of you bragging about beating me on these streets. Do yourself a favor and stay humble." I nodded to indicate my understanding and then signaled to my friends that it was time to go.

After that day, we never ventured into that park again. I must admit that I was rattled and couldn't help but wonder what might have transpired if Al had made his shot or if I had missed. There were other parks where my friends and I could dominate, and, as my father had once wisely said, "I could live to play another day."

Dread

After completing another day at work, I head to my car to embark on the journey home. While many people anticipate this time of day as the moment when work concludes, even enduring the traffic seems preferable to extending the workday by another hour. Our schedules demand early starts and end precisely amidst the evening traffic peak. Let me clarify, I do appreciate my job and feel grateful to have it.

Having experienced a layoff from my previous job after a decade of service, landing this new job felt like a true blessing. Thus, the challenging aspect of my day doesn't stem from the job itself, despite its potential stressors. Neither is it the grueling standstill traffic. The most arduous part of my day awaits me at home. It's disheartening when the prospect of returning home fills me with dread, mainly because he will be there, inevitably consumed by anger.

His disposition was consistently clouded with rage, and seldom did it appear justified. My late mother had attempted to caution me, her words echoing, "Child, that man finds no happy unless he's mad. Be cautious around someone like him, as he'll cast his misery onto your soul. In time, this will only leave you exasperated, leaving behind a bitter aftertaste."

Regrettably, I didn't heed my mother's advice, swayed by the love I held for him. During the periods when his disgruntlement and fury subsided, he could transform into the wittiest individual alive. He had an uncanny ability to discover humor even in the most peculiar situations, and his laughter resonated deeply, resounding like a bell. There were moments when I'd simply observe him, pondering how a man with such a hearty laugh could harbor such cruelty.

I remained by his side, driven by my personal motivations, some of which were self-centered. He excelled as a provider, a point he frequently emphasized, and he genuinely cared for our children. Nonetheless, a sinister aspect of him existed, eclipsing the intensity of a category five hurricane over the warm Gulf of Mexico waters. Swiftly and without apparent cause, his moods would shift, and he'd descend into fussing. His state of mind seemed persistently on edge and irritable. It took mere moments for him to delve into my flaws and failures, conveniently omitting any of his own.

Having persevered through the congested traffic and gradual slow-downs, I finally turn into the driveway. As I pull in, I notice the curtains drawn apart in the front window, facing the street. There he stands, pacing back and forth as if trapped like an animal in a zoo enclosure. The aura around him practically exudes steam, reminiscent of a bull ready to charge. Amidst his pacing, he's glued to his phone, his lips moving rapidly. Something must have occurred, triggering his volatile emotions once again.

Before I step out of the car and enter the house, I take a moment to sit and gather myself. It's clear that nothing but turmoil and disharmony awaits me inside, and today, I'm in no state of mind to deal with it. This is my reality, a reality I've permitted to take root around me, and now it feels as though it's enveloping me entirely.

Wrong Place Wrong Time

Funerals have always been difficult for me to deal with. This funeral is even more intense because it is the funeral of my father. My father suffered from a vicious disease that ultimately took his life. The past two years have been particularly trying for me because I turned over my business to my business partner to spend more time with my father. I am not complaining, not in the least, because those last two years saw my relationship with him grow closer and closer.

I always knew he was proud of me, but during that time, he shared so much about himself that I was unaware of. He shared his ups and downs and the mistakes he made. He talked at great length about his love for my mother and how he wished he could go back and change some things in his past. I never pressed the issue because it was his time to open up and be honest. Those last two years were a blessing for me, and I am convinced they were a blessing for him as well.

His funeral was well-planned, and the turnout exceeded my expectations. I recognized just about everyone here, except for a few people who worked with my father. While I didn't know them by facial recognition, once they introduced themselves, I felt like I knew them in detail. My father would often discuss the people at his job with great admiration, so I was able to account for everyone at the funeral except for one lone individual. This man had caught my eye for some reason. He was neatly dressed in a dark blue suit with a pocket square and a tightly tied tie. At first, I thought he might be associated with the people from my father's job, but he didn't seem to interact with any of them. I dismissed it and didn't think too much of it until I saw my uncle go up to him and give him a hug.

I found this particularly strange because my uncle was not the hugging type of person. He could be testy at times, and at other times, he was downright boorish. Yet, there he was, giving this guy a hug. I dismissed this thought again and settled into my seat for the start of the service. The minister spoke glowing words about my father, which I appreciated, considering he had only known my father for the past two years. My father was never one to go to church or cozy up to a preacher. I once heard him tell my uncle, "Don't let any preacher near your house. I'm telling you, if you let him near your house, eventually he will be keeping time with your wife while you're at work."

Thinking of that statement brought a smile to my face due to the irony of the situation. My father had never had time for a preacher, but over the last two years, he had grown fond of this one. To mask my giggling face, I turned away from the preacher. When I turned toward the congregation, I noticed the nicely dressed guy with a smirk on his face. It was as if we were sharing the same private joke. I also observed that he was sitting next to my Aunt Ruby. They weren't sitting next to each other like strangers do, with an agreed space between them. Aunt Ruby was sitting pretty close to him, and I think I saw her grab his hand and give it a caress.

My giggles were now turning into a state of confusion. Who is this guy, and why does it seem like he fits in but not really fitting in? I turned to take another glance at him, and I began to notice that we shared similar facial features as well. Our noses were broad and wide, and we both had high cheekbones. My second glance at him must have caught my mother's attention because she grabbed my hand and said, "Son, what is so interesting to you that you're not paying attention to the minister's words?"

I looked at my mother and said, "Mother, you're right. This is our last time with my father, and I don't need to be distracted. By the way, do you see that guy back there sitting close to Aunt Ruby? Do you know him? Is he related to us, maybe a cousin I wasn't aware of?" I chuckled to lighten the mood with my mother. Then I continued, "He almost looks like our side of the family. Look at that bell pepper-sized nose and those high cheekbones. If I didn't know any better, I would swear he was related to us."

My mother grabbed my shoulders and turned me toward the minister as he was wrapping up his sermon. Just as the minister said, "At this time, I would like the immediate family to come forward and get a final look at their loved one before the casket is closed." My family was no longer a large one, and most of the elders had passed on, while the younger relatives lived in different states. I wasn't expecting a crowd at the casket. I got up and helped my mother to her feet. As I made my way to the aisle, I let my mother go ahead of me. Just as I was about to head to the casket, the well-dressed young man bumped into me.

I couldn't help but wonder why he was heading up there. Didn't he hear the minister say that this time was for the immediate family? I gave him a sour look, and in return, he gave me a slight smile. He extended his hand as if offering me the right of way toward the casket. I buttoned my suit button and said to him, "Excuse me, sir, but this time is for immediate family. You might want to go back to your seat."

He gave me another slight smile and extended his hand toward my back as if he were ushering me to the casket. He whispered to me, "It will all be okay. We will talk afterwards."

"We will talk afterward!" I thought, bewildered. Who is this guy, and why is he up here with the immediate family? The minister instructed everyone to bow their heads and say a silent prayer for my father. I bowed my head but slightly opened my right eye, only to notice this guy standing next to me with his head bowed. I quickly closed my right eye and turned to my left, where my mother was standing. I slightly opened my left eye to see if my mother was witnessing the same thing, but she only squeezed my hand a little harder.

After the moment of prayer, we returned to our seats, but I couldn't help myself. I continued to turn around and steal glances at this mystery figure. I had trouble concentrating on the funeral because my attention was now fixated on this enigmatic individual. I turned to my mother once again, but before I could say anything, she said, "Son, fix your tie and pay attention. We only have a few more minutes of this service, and then it will all be over. Your father will officially be with the saints in Heaven."

As the service wrapped up and we all headed toward the hearse waiting to take my father to the gravesite, I turned back to look for the guy, and lo and behold, he was standing right behind me. I stared into his eyes with an intense gaze and said, "What is it with you? Do you usually just show up at funerals and pretend to be part of a family? By the way, who are you, and what business did you have with my father?"

Before he could open his mouth to answer me, my Uncle approached and said, "Why don't you two guys get in the family limousine and let the driver take you to the gravesite. It's a short ride down to Gentilly Boulevard, but that will give you two some time to get introduced and share a word or two."

I turned to my Uncle with an angry look on my face and said, "What is wrong with everyone today? You're all acting strangely, and we have a well-dressed stranger creeping up behind me on the day of my father's funeral. Once we get to the repast, someone is going to explain to me what is going on!" After those words, I stormed off to the limousine and started to get in. Just as I was closing the door, the strange guy stopped the door from closing and sat in the car next to me. He shut the door and told the driver that we were ready to head to the gravesite. He turned to me and said, "Brother, we have to talk, but not until we bury our father."

I gave him the most perplexed look I could muster and yelled back, "Brother?!"

Life

My mother used to say, "When it rains, it pours." I have come to believe in that statement now, even though I never paid too much attention to it when I used to hear it. I am in my childhood bedroom, lying in my old bed at my parents' house. It is much smaller than I remember; my old room now feels like a jail cell. When I was a kid, my room seemed vast, as if I could fit the entire world in it. But now, I'm in a state of depression because no grown man wants to be back in his parents' house. The whole idea of being a grown-up is to get out on your own, establish your own life, and it's disheartening to return to the place you started from.

The downturn in the economy has affected me in numerous ways. I lost my job due to downsizing after spending over 10 years with a major corporation. My job was eliminated, and according to a former co-worker, my assistant now occupies what used to be my office. I tried to stay in the city, keeping my head up and going on interview after interview, but no one was hiring. I did receive a few offers, but when you've been making a six-figure salary, it's difficult to accept a job that starts at twenty-five thousand a year. I thought about using my retirement and savings to get by for a while until things improved, but the economic downturn also led to a decline in the stock market. My retirement fund and savings were now worth very little, having taken a more significant punch than a prizefighter.

I knew I couldn't support my family or our lifestyle on my wife's income alone; it simply wasn't enough. She was a school teacher, and while her wages always provided extras for our household, we never relied on them to survive. Our two sons attended private school and were accustomed to a comfortable life.

After losing our house to foreclosure and struggling to find employment, I was at a loss for what to do next. It was then that my mother reached out to check on us and proposed a brilliant idea. She offered us the opportunity to move into her house, the very same house I had grown up in. Since my father's passing, she had been living alone in the house. The decision was made and relayed to me without my input, following yet another day of unsuccessful job hunting. Not only had I not been part of this decision, but my wife had already organized our belongings to be packed, and the moving company would soon be in the process of loading our things into a moving van.

Amid the whirlwind of change, my wife explained that it was time to let go of our deferred dreams and face reality. She assured me that moving back to my parents' house would be temporary and that once the economy improved, we could consider returning to the city. Her words were comforting, yet I couldn't ignore the inkling that she had embraced the idea of leaving the city behind for good. Unlike the hustle and status-consciousness of the urban lifestyle, she had never truly connected with it. Her strength shone through in any setting, but she didn't flaunt anything except our children's achievements. Thus, relocating to the countryside aligned perfectly with her preferences, and she was eager to embark on this new chapter of our lives.

Moving to a different location is one challenge, but considering the state of the economy, I could only imagine what it would be like in a small rural town. Surprisingly, my wife had already secured a teaching job. Somehow, my mother had connections with the school superintendent, and she reached out to inquire about teaching opportunities. As expected, my wife had a job waiting for her before we even arrived in the town. My mother appeared to have an extensive network, spanning friends, family, and church members. She had a knack for invoking my father's name when seeking substantial favors, and it seemed like doors opened effortlessly, granting her access to all she needed.

I make my way to the kitchen to see what's happening, only to realize that the kids are already at school and my wife is at work. I wonder why I've been sleeping in so late and what I've been doing with my time. My mother has prepared a full breakfast for me, and she warmly embraces me with a hug and a kiss that only a mother can give. She assures me that everything will be alright and attributes my state to a mild bout of depression. Though I attempt to protest, my words fall on deaf ears because, as we all know, mother knows best. She likens my current state of depression to the times when I faced heartbreak or loss in the past – like when Theresa Washington broke up with me before prom, or when we lost in the high school state championship game. According to her, these bouts of depression come and go, but they're transient as long as they're replaced by moments of joy. We sit together at the table as I enjoy my breakfast, and her eyes are filled with a profound love and understanding.

As I'm still eating, my mother mentions that Mr. Zach dropped by earlier in the morning after hearing about my return to town. Mr. Zach was not only my father's best friend but also his colleague. Although he worked under my father, my dad never considered it that way; he always insisted that they worked together, as friends should. My dad owned a lawn service, and that's the only job I ever saw him do. He and Mr. Zach would head out every morning in his pickup truck with a trailer hitched to the back, loaded with all the necessary equipment, water coolers, and salt tablets. While I couldn't quite comprehend how he made a living cutting grass, my parents never lacked for anything. They led a simple but comfortable life, and their needs were always met.

I noticed my mother trying to hide a book behind her back, her demeanor a bit uneasy. She confessed that she hadn't been accustomed to handling my father's business matters, but his passing left her with no choice. She handed me my father's business records and asked me to examine the numbers. To my surprise, my father had been making a very substantial income from his lawn care business. I'm talking about a substantial income that could sustain him during both the busy summer months and the leaner winter period. My dad was never one to boast about his earnings, so this revelation caught me off guard. My mother mentioned that Mr. Zach would be returning the following morning for breakfast, and I couldn't help but give her a skeptical look, wondering if there was anything between them. She assured me that he would be pulling out all the old equipment and making sure it was in working order.

Around this time of year, my dad and Mr. Zach would always get the equipment out and test it for the upcoming cutting season. I didn't think much of it until my mother informed me that she had told Mr. Zach that I would be taking over my dad's business, which is why I returned home. "Mom, why did you say that? And why would you lie to Mr. Zach like that? I have no intention of making a living by mowing lawns, no matter how much money Dad made from it. I'm a college graduate, and as soon as the economy picks up, I'm going back to my profession in New Orleans. Let Mr. Zach have the business if he wants it, but I didn't go to college just to cut grass."

My mother's voice, usually soft and gentle, took on a stern tone as she responded, "Son, never disrespect the memory of your father, my husband. He worked tirelessly to ensure that both you and I had everything we needed. Did you ever think about how you were able to go to college without worrying about tuition? Or where the down payment for your first home came from? Never forget the memory of your father, who was a great man—may his soul rest in peace!" Tears welled in her eyes as I moved closer to offer a hug, and a flood of memories of my dad overwhelmed me. I reminisced about eagerly awaiting his phone calls and how he'd send me fresh fish caught during his fishing trips with Mr. Zach. I remembered his late-night conversations about sports and life, and how he'd prepared me for so many aspects of life.

Just as I felt a tear welling up, my mother instructed me to go to my room and prepare to make some phone calls. She wanted me to contact all of my dad's former clients and let them know I would be taking over his business and inquired if they would consider being my clients once more. The first call I made was to my wife. When she called me back, there was silence on the other end. I shared the morning's events, expressing my frustration at my mother's attempt to map out my future. I emphasized that despite her good intentions, I am a grown man who won't allow anyone to dictate my life choices. Silence persisted on the line. Annoyed, I asked my wife if she had heard what I said, but she softly replied that taking over my dad's business might not be a bad idea. She explained that I needed an activity to keep me engaged, especially since our sons had been concerned about me. She advised me to take the day to think it over and teased that she had a surprise for me when she returned home.

I'm not a fan of surprises, so I implored her to reveal it right away. After another pause, she gently revealed that she had bought me work shirts, jeans, and work boots. Before I could protest, she informed me she had to get back to work, expressed her love, and her belief in me. It became evident that my wife and mother had been discussing things while I slept. They had concocted a scheme to rejuvenate my dad's business, with me at the helm. This wasn't part of my plan, and I had no intention of going along with it. Although I had no solid plans at the moment, one thing was certain: I wouldn't be spending my days mowing lawns.

Later in the day, as my wife entered the house, I braced myself for a verbal confrontation with these two assertive women. Just as I was ready to engage, my wife enveloped me in a hug and handed me the bag of work clothes, instructing me to try them on. As I looked up to express my opposition, the faces of my sons mirrored the same sense of pride I remembered when I used to see my dad coming home from a hard day's work. In that moment, I realized I had to hold off on the argument for the sake of my sons. But I was firm – I would not be mowing lawns for a living.

After a night filled with uneasy silence between my wife and me, I woke up to a jarring sight. Mr. Zach sat at my bedside, watching me. He informed me that the equipment was in good shape, but the pickup needed a tune-up, and I needed to go with him to the auto shop. I questioned why he couldn't handle it himself and I could just provide the money. He reminded me that he didn't drive, and this was something my dad would have handled. He also reminded me that my mother had breakfast ready and that he would be waiting in the truck. Frustrated, I exclaimed, "Doesn't anyone in this town listen?!" First my mother, then my wife, and now Mr. Zach – was this some kind of mystery movie episode where people could see me but not hear me?

Heading to the kitchen, my mother greeted me with a hug and a kiss, urging me to eat my breakfast and not keep Mr. Zach waiting in the truck. With determination in her voice, she said, "Son, I don't want to hear about your plans or objections. Take this check and take the truck for a tune-up. While you're there, take this contract to Mr. Johnson, who owns the auto shop. He might be a bit irritated because I told him you'd come by yesterday, but if you offer to mow his lawn for free this one time, he'll be fine." She swiftly took away the breakfast plate after just one bite and insisted that life was waiting for me to embrace, urging me to move forward.

My mother informs me that Mr. Zach will provide me with information about the regular customers and which ones I should visit today. At this point, I'm realizing that reasoning with my mother might be futile, so I begin to hope that Mr. Zach will be more understanding of my predicament. Climbing into my dad's truck, Mr. Zach proceeds to explain the routine of the business. He emphasizes that I need to adopt a sense of urgency if I'm going to succeed in this field. I take the opportunity to express to Mr. Zach that I have no intention of taking over my dad's business and that I'm willing to donate the equipment and the truck to him if he's interested. Once again, Mr. Zach pays little attention to my words, instead urging me to step up and make my dad proud once more.

While we wait for the truck to be serviced, I review the business records and the customer list. A thought crosses my mind – perhaps I could serve as a consultant to Mr. Zach and assist him in taking over the business. I decide to call my wife at work to discuss the idea and gather her opinion. Following a brief silence, she softly responds, "I am proud of you, and I have confidence in you." I begin to wonder if anyone is truly listening to my intentions and concerns.

Finally, the truck is ready, and as Mr. Johnson approaches with the keys, he eyes me up and down, sizing me up. Handing over the keys, he informs me that his Centennial roses are growing uncontrollably, while his Green Ice Boxwood is withering. He questions my plan of action or whether he should call the Hicks brothers to take over his landscaping. Deliberately, I present the contract to him and ask him to review it before making a decision. Mr. Johnson states that he won't pay a 10% increase due to the economic downturn, but he's willing to accept a 5% raise. After reviewing the contract, he instructs me to have my mother make the necessary adjustments and send him the revised version. He adds, "Now, please take care of my lawn and bushes before my clients think I've closed shop." I've stepped into the deep end of the pool – I'm now bound by a legal contract with a business owner, and I'm compelled to uphold my end of the agreement. It seems that I've unexpectedly entered the world of the lawn service business.

As Mr. Zach and I head back towards the house, I notice a sign on Joe's Plumbing lawn that reads "LAWN SERVICE DONE BY HICKS BROTHERS." Mr. Zach turns to me, his tone serious, and explains that this is our competition and we need to step up our efforts to survive. He brings up a memory from high school, asking if I remember Gerry Hicks, one of the Hicks brothers, who played basketball alongside me. Memories rush back – Gerry was our star player, and I was the starting point guard during that pivotal state championship game. We lost that crucial match, and I made a critical turnover in the game's final moments. Gerry held me responsible, and his anger was echoed by his father in a local newspaper article that criticized my performance. Over the years, their resentment grew as Gerry's basketball aspirations were dashed, and he ended up playing for a small college before an injury curtailed his career. Their bitterness linked back to that championship game, and I became the target of their unfulfilled dreams. Once I moved away, I lost touch with Gerry and our other teammates, but it seems he remained in town and joined his family's business.

Mr. Zach directs me to make a sudden right turn and stop at Mr. Alex's Barbershop. Although I don't believe I need a haircut, Mr. Zach insists he needs a quick trim, and so we stop unexpectedly. To my surprise, the truck bearing the name "HICKS LAWN SERVICE" is parked right outside the barbershop. Suddenly, Mr. Zach doesn't appear to be in need of a trim; rather, he seems to be seeking additional motivation to stoke his competitive spirit. As we enter the barbershop, Mr. Alex greets me with a loud voice, referencing the reunion of the "most famous backcourt in the history of this community." Gerry stands to shake my hand but holds on tightly, looking at me with disdain. He shares his desire to look into the eyes of the person who prevented him from reaching the pros. His brothers burst into laughter, and his father seems ready for confrontation. It's clear that time hasn't healed the wounds of the past for them. Gerry and his brothers have taken over the family lawn business and are determined to dominate the local lawn care industry.

As I sit and take in the surroundings, I notice that the Hicks brothers are dressed identically – the same color work pants, boots, and work shirts with their company logo and names. Clearly, the lawn service business has evolved since my younger days. Mr. Alex inquires with the Hicks brothers about landscaping his new home, and Gerry efficiently uses a handheld computer to discuss his appointments. The world of lawn care has embraced technology, and now it's time for me to step up and honor my dad's legacy.

Later that evening as we gathered around the large kitchen table for another of my mother's dinners, I feel compelled to make an announcement. I interrupt the meal to declare that I'm officially taking over the family lawn service business. My sons share high fives, my wife tears up, and my mother embraces me tightly. I express the need for their support and admit that returning to our previous lifestyle might be challenging, but I'm committed to giving it my all. My wife pledges her support, and my sons propose handling record-keeping and appointment updates using the computer. My mother informs me that she has untouched funds from my father that I can use, and she believes I'll use them wisely. I call Mr. Zach to share my decision and ask him to be at the house the next morning. His humorous response is that he's not going anywhere at 5 am anyway.

Now, I'm ready to work anew. I've discovered a passion not just for making money, but for continuing my father's legacy. My passion is fueled by the determination to show my sons that their father can thrive in any situation and support them. It's driven by the desire to prove to the woman who believes in me that I'm worthy of her admiration. It's also motivated by the goal of demonstrating to the Hicks brothers that the young man who struggled on the biggest stage has grown into a capable adversary.

My mother's words about depression visiting briefly and its departure being determined by one's outlook resonate with me. I might have let depression linger a bit too long, but now I'm refocused and ready to confront life head-on. I'm dedicated, motivated, and even energized in my pursuit to rejuvenate the business and, in the process, revitalize myself.

Beloved

Life is filled with surprises, and sometimes those surprises can knock you off your feet. Such was the case for me. The last place you expect to see an old flame is at a parade. I loved going to the night parades; the majesty of the floats, the bright lights, and the sound of the marching bands are some of my favorite parts of living in New Orleans. Parades are gatherings of family and friends, and you're bound to see someone you know. It may be a coworker, a former teacher, or even someone you had disagreements with in the past. The last person you want to see at a parade, having the time of their life, is an old flame. Yet, there she was.

We met in high school. I needed to fill my schedule with an elective class. There wasn't much to choose from since most of the athletes took easier classes like art or home economics. So, I was left with taking a book club class. We would be assigned two books to read, and our assignment was to discuss the books as well. We had conversations about how we interpreted the books or how we felt about the writer's point of view.

It was something I wasn't really interested in, but I had to have a full schedule, so I sucked it up and attended. On the first day of class, I ended up arriving a few minutes late. The hallway was crowded, and it didn't help that the football team was slowly moving toward the locker room. I tried to ease by, but I was met with unintentional elbows or sudden nudges from players who were too large to be in high school.

As I entered the class, the instructor took a moment to address my tardiness. "Welcome to class, sir. I'm thrilled that you could join us, but in the future, if you're going to attend this class, let's make sure you're on time." As I began to explain to the instructor why I was late, he cut me off mid-sentence and, with a firm voice, said, "No excuses, just be on time."

I made my way to the back of the class and plopped down into a chair. My disinterest in taking this class was already established when I reluctantly signed up, but now it was elevated by a brutish instructor. A copy of the book we were supposed to read was sitting on the desk, waiting for my arrival. With halfhearted interest, I picked it up and opened it to the beginning. The instructor declared in a loud, dispassionate voice, "Class, your first assignment is to read the first three chapters of the book. I also want you to be able to tell me at least three things about the author of the book. Make sure you come to class tomorrow having read the first three chapters. I will spend our time today telling you three things about the author. So, half of your homework assignment is going to be done for you."

It was then that I felt a hand touch my shoulder, and there she was. She was tall and beautiful, her skin a radiant brown, and her eyes brimming with life. Her smile was warm and inviting, and she seemed to have a certain aura about her. She said, "Hey, I took this class last year, so I have all of the notes if you're interested."

At first, I was at a loss for words. I had seen just about every girl in school, but I was sure I had never seen her. She was absolutely gorgeous. I mustered up the strength to respond, "Why are you taking the class again? Did you fail it last year?"

She gave me a whimsical look and said, "No, I didn't fail the class, silly. I happen to like books and discussing them, so I took the class again. I can help you if you want, but if you think you're not going to need my help, that's understandable."

At this point, we had both tuned out the instructor, and I accepted her offer to help. That's where our relationship started. We would meet during lunch breaks in the courtyard and discuss the assignments, exchanging ideas. I had never met such an intelligent person with so much insight. I was captivated by her beauty and her ability to break down the assignments in a way that even someone like me, who felt lost, could make sense of it.

After a month of classes and a few passing grades, I found the courage to ask her out. She said she didn't go out too often, but we could start meeting at her house after school. She told me to make sure I brought my books because her parents weren't going to tolerate me just sitting on their sofa making out. So, we began to meet after school at her house. We would read and discuss the assigned books, and she would help me with homework.

Gradually, our discussions about assignments evolved into conversations about life, love, and passion. I was still amazed by her beauty and taken aback by her intellect. She was, by far, the smartest person I knew in my age group. Eventually, we started making out, and we spent every available moment together. We fell in love, becoming passionate and intimate with each other.

Our relationship continued for two years until it was time to graduate. She had plans to attend an out-of-state women's college. I had no concrete plans. She suggested that I attend the local Community College just to see how I liked college life. I wanted to suggest attending a college near where she was going, but I never did. There was a part of me that longed for her to make that suggestion, but she never did.

She went off to college, and it was as if she had vanished from my world. No letters or phone calls came. I didn't want to reach out to her, fearing it might come across as desperation. So, I gave her space and time to potentially miss me, but that scenario never seemed to unfold. I waited until Christmas break and asked her parents if she was planning to come home. Her dad informed me that she wasn't returning home. They believed it was better for her to stay at school during the break, avoiding frequent travel.

That marked the last time I inquired about her with her parents. I let go of the idea of her and our relationship. I considered it a high school romance that she had likely outgrown. That was four years ago, and since then, I had moved on with my life.

Mardi gras season was in full swing, and I was in a relationship with a wonderful woman a few years older than me. She wasn't originally from New Orleans, so she relished the parades even more than I did.

The floats continued to glide by as the bands played on, and I found myself looking around, struck by the way a single event could elicit so much joy from such a diverse crowd. A momentary pause in the parade occurred as one of the floats lagged behind. Seizing that instant, I turned my gaze across the street into the throng of onlookers. Initially, I hesitated, not entirely sure of what my eyes were registering. Yet, there she stood – a few years older, exuding maturity, yet undeniably her. I couldn't help but gaze, a sliver of hope flickering inside me that she might spot me amidst the crowd. I stood there captivated, observing her from a distance. Her beautiful smile emerged, the very smile etched in my memory. For a fleeting second, it felt like her smile was directed at me, but soon enough, I realized her smile was meant for someone else.

A tempest of emotions surged within me, all the while I endeavored to conceal them from my girlfriend's notice. The parade resumed its progression, yet my focus remained steadfastly fixed across the street. A part of me yearned to bridge the distance, to summon the courage to approach her and deliver the lines I had rehearsed for years. My mind raced. Should I gather the audacity to venture over and initiate a conversation? Would she perhaps recognize me and initiate contact? Would my girlfriend discern my preoccupation and start probing?

The parade marched forward, while my mind wrestled with an internal conflict between the past and the present – a quandary I hadn't braced myself to confront.

I attempted to pull myself together, redirecting my focus back to the parade and my girlfriend, who was thoroughly enjoying herself. Yet, my gaze kept drifting across the street. My stomach was twisted into knots, and my thoughts were in disarray. Could I have been mistaken in believing we once shared a love? Was my affection one-sided? It seemed inconceivable to me that someone could abruptly sever all communication with someone they once loved.

Just as I was getting lost in my contemplations, my girlfriend interrupted my reverie by waving her hand in front of my face. "Hey, that's the last float. Let's get ready to leave. Are you okay? You've seemed distant for the past hour or so."

I assured her that I was fine, but as we prepared to depart, I stole one last glance across the street. She was still there, and this time, it appeared as though she was looking at me. She gave me that familiar smile and raised her hand slightly above her waist, offering a slow wave – the kind of wave meant for just the two of us, not for anyone else to see. I longed to respond, to cross the street, embrace her, maybe even share a kiss. I yearned for answers about why she vanished from my life. I sought closure, unknowingly neglecting the fact that she had already provided that closure when she departed for college. I craved understanding as to why she chose to leave me without explanation.

Instead, I shifted my focus and clasped my girlfriend's hand. Her excitement over the parade was palpable. She chatted animatedly about the lights, the bands, and every detail she managed to glean from the floats. While she poured out her enthusiasm, I listened with a partial ear, my attention still tangled up in the evening's unfolding. The sight of the woman who had once held my heart continued to play on my mind, throwing me off balance.

I was doing my girlfriend a disservice by only half-engaging in our conversation, all the while still entangled in the emotions of the night. The image of a woman I had once believed I loved remained a persistent presence, casting a shadow over my current moment.

Incomplete

I've heard people say that a mother's love is unlike anything else. I guess I'm one of those people who hasn't experienced that. It's not because I don't have a mother – oh, I definitely have one. It's because my mother seems stuck in a state of arrested development.

My mother had just turned eighteen when I was born. I never knew or heard about my daddy, and she never brought him up. My mother was thrust into parenthood at a young age, and she resisted it every step of the way. She took on various jobs to keep a roof over our heads and put fast food on the table. But being a mother was never her priority. She always said that we would grow up as pals, but I didn't want or need a friend. What I wanted and needed was a mother – someone to nurture and care for me, to guide me in the right direction and help me navigate this world.

Her youth wasn't an excuse, as there were other young mothers in our neighborhood. I would see them strolling with their kids or enjoying games together, but I never got to experience that. Whenever I asked my mother to go for a walk or play catch, she'd just say, "Boy, I've got better things to do with my time. Now go find something to do. There are other kids outside – go play with them."

She seemed to overlook the fact that I was a shy kid and making friends wasn't easy for me. On top of that, I was overweight. So while the other kids were biking and racing around, I was the one struggling to keep up. I ended up staying indoors, watching the other kids play from morning till night.

My interests weren't her top priority, or even a concern of hers. Her free time was spent entertaining, smoking and drinking. I'd see strangers in our house who somehow knew my name. Sometimes, I'd run into one of them in the morning on their way to the bathroom. They'd wake up groggy and ruffle their afros. "Hey lil man, does your mother keep any coffee around here?"

Those seemed to be the only interactions I'd have with them. They were strangers, so I never really talked to them or asked about their names.

Sometimes, my mother would wake up around the same time, a cigarette dangling from her mouth, and pour cereal into a bowl for me. There were many mornings when we didn't have any milk to pour over the cereal. Her usual excuse was that she meant to buy milk but got sidetracked by something. That excuse started to wear thin on me.

One morning, she asked one of her friends to take me to the store to buy some milk. I wasn't too comfortable getting into a car with a guy I had only just met a few minutes ago, but there I was, on the way to the store. As I coughed in the midst of his cigarette smoke, he turned to me and said, "So kid, do you even have a name? Your mother always refers to you as 'her boy,' without attaching a name to you. Everyone has a name."

Just as I was about to answer, he interrupted, saying, "Boy, your mother is something else. She's got a fiery spirit and doesn't hold back her words. But you know what, that's what I admire about her — that little temper of hers."

As we pulled into the store's parking lot, I stayed in the car, staring at the store window. "Well, boy, are you going to get out and grab the milk? Come on, I've got things to do, and I can't hang around all day."

I turned reluctantly to the man, still unaware of his name, and told him that I needed money. "I don't have any money; I thought you were going to give me money for the milk."

The man looked both confused and disgusted, saying, "Boy, if you thought I was buying you milk, you must be out of your mind. Let me make this clear — I'm not your father, and I'm definitely not your mother's boyfriend. I'm just some random guy she met at work. So why would you think I'd buy you milk? I'm taking you back home, and you can sort this out with your mother."

He turned the car around and drove me back. He didn't even come inside; he just left me at the front door. I walked in, still hungry and with my head down. My mother was awake now, tidying the front room. "Boy, where's the milk? I sent you to the store for milk. That cereal is going to taste awful without any milk."

"Boy, I'm talking to you. I asked you a question. Don't just stand there looking like an idiot. Talk to me – I asked you something!"

Before I could reply, tears started rolling down my cheeks. Inside, I felt utterly helpless, but I didn't know how to convey those emotions to her. I lacked the words to express the pain and emptiness that I had been feeling for a while now.

My mother yelled at me, "Boy, I guess you're just going to stand there crying like a baby. Go to the kitchen and fix yourself a bowl of dry cereal. I don't have time for this; I have to work at noon. Plus, I'm throwing a house party tonight, so stay in your room and only come out if you need the bathroom."

With those words, I made my way to the kitchen for a bowl of cereal without any milk. Left alone, I tried to make sense of my emotions at such a young age. I had no idea what it meant to be a parent, but I knew that this situation wasn't right. This was all I had ever known, but deep in my heart, I believed there was more to life than a house filled with strangers and bowls of cereal without milk.

Let Down

Christmas was always a time of good cheer, presents, and big announcements. This year, I planned for Christmas to be one for the ages. My girlfriend and I had been living together for two years now, and it was time to pop the question. I wasn't sure how I would approach the subject, but I knew I had to follow my heart and ask her to marry me.

It was Christmas Eve, and the time to pop the question was so near that I began to shake. This would mark a big step in my life and lead me down a road to marriage that I had never considered with anyone else. She was locked in the bedroom, on her computer getting her work completed. There was a sign on the bedroom door letting me know not to disturb her. My excitement was overwhelming, and I couldn't wait, so I knocked ever so gently on the door. "Hey, it's me. I know you said you were busy, but I have something for you. It will only take a minute or two. Can you consider unlocking the door, please?"

Before I could finish my statement, I could hear her sighing in disgust. She stormed to the door to unlock it, and when she opened the door, she said in a huff, "What is it! My goodness, the note on the door said it, and yet you still knock and interrupt me. Do you think I want to work on Christmas Eve? Well, I don't, but here I am, and you can't seem to follow simple instructions on the bedroom door, so what is it that can't wait?"

I was so excited about the moment that I put her coarse disposition aside. I mustered up courage that I knew was buried deep down inside and spoke, "Hey, I know you're busy, but I wanted to take a moment to talk to you about something."

With those words, I pulled out the small brown box that held the engagement ring and began to bend down on one knee. Just as I was about to open the box and request her hand in marriage, she stopped me in my tracks. With a quizzical look on her face and even a slight smile, she uttered, "Boy, now I know you're not about to pop the question! Please, please tell me that you're not about to do that. Let me take a look at that ring. That is a nice ring, but that is something you would give a high school girlfriend. That little thing can't even catch the light from the overhead light. Where did you get that from and who sold you that little diamond?"

At first, my feelings were a little bruised, but I am a fighter so I am not going to let a few words bother me. I was determined to ask the proposal question and leave the rest up to her. Just as I was about to open my mouth and ask the big question, I paused and said, "What do you mean the ring looks like something you would give a high school girlfriend? I worked hard and a lot of overtime to be able to put this ring on your finger. I have three years of payments to remind me of how hard I worked and will be working for this ring. So how could you be so dismissive when I haven't even asked you the big question yet?"

With a disinterested look on her face, she gave a devilish smile and responded, "Look, I don't know if you've been paying attention, but I want so much more than a tiny apartment and a ring that you're going to be paying for the next three years. I want a life like my friend Shawn. She is engaged to a professional football player. She has a three-carat ring, and he just bought her a new car. That is the life I want to live, not some barely getting by life. Have you seen Shawn's house? That thing is enormous and has everything in it. That is the life I want, so the answer to the question is going to be No Thank You!"

With those words, she slammed the door to the bedroom and went back to working on her computer. To say I was stunned is an understatement. To say I was crushed doesn't even begin to describe my feelings. I walked away from the bedroom door with a broken heart. I had to remind myself that I am a fighter and I am not going to let a few coarse words destroy my plans.

Brokenhearted, I turned around and headed back to the bedroom and knocked on the door once again. "Hey, take some time to think about it and get back to me. I know the holidays are a stressful time for all of us, and I might have taken you by surprise with the whole ring thing. So take a day or two, and let's discuss it as we head into the New Year."

The bedroom door flew open, and this time she seemed to be in even more of a rage. "I told you already that I don't want that bubble gum ring. I hope you kept your receipt so you can bring that little thing back to the store. I am not sure how dense one person can be, but you're dense. Not only am I not going to marry you, but Shawn is on her way here with one of her boyfriend's teammates. He plays on the team and drives a one-hundred-thousand-dollar car. His chain around his wrist is worth more than you make in three years, and plus, dude is famous. He is really famous, like he is on television every Sunday. Can you compare to that, can you compare to him?"

Hearing those words destroyed me on the inside. I have never known her to be so harsh. I knew she had her moods from time to time, but nothing like this. Not only was she rejecting my proposal and the ring, but she is now telling me that she is going out with another guy. This is Christmas Eve, and she is doing this to me. As I contemplated all this and tried to digest the happening of the moment, something came over me that I had not experienced ever in my life. I was usually the most even-keeled person you would want to know. There was very little drama in my life, and I got along fine with all my neighbors and all of her friends. Yet, even-keeled is not what I am feeling right now.

What I am feeling right now is rage and rejection. I would usually take this all in and just hope for a better day, but today is different. I don't know if it is the holidays or if I have just had enough. I go to the bedroom door and swing it wide open. Just as I am about to give her a piece of my mind, she brushes past me in a hurry. She is dressed in her long coat that I bought her, and she has her face all adorned in makeup. I run ahead of her, preventing her from leaving out of the door, and with all the rage I can muster, I say, "Hey, let's talk this over. I am sure we can work on this, and I promise I will get you another ring."

She brushes right past me and runs toward a guy who, even from a distance, is an enormous human being. I have never seen a hundred-thousand-dollar car up close, but he certainly has one. I watch from the balcony as she drives away with all my hopes and dreams. I go back into the apartment and pray that she is safe and hopefully we can talk about this once she comes back home. Merry Christmas.

Nights

My mother used to tell me in her kindest voice, "Son, you're a peculiar child." She would speak those words and always conclude with a big smile. She knew I wasn't like my brothers and sisters who enjoyed partying and having a good time. I was more of a homebody, someone who found joy in reading a good book.

I would settle on the front porch of our home and crack open a good book. Sometimes it was a book that I needed to read for schoolwork, and other times it was a magazine about sports. I was known for having a book with me most of the time, especially at night. I would take advantage of the tranquility of the night to immerse myself in the words on the pages. My routine was to apply lotion to my arms and legs so that mosquitoes wouldn't bother me. As I sat down to read, my brothers and sisters would rush past me without even pausing as they walked down the steps. They would leap off the porch and head to the nearest house party or sometimes to the corner barroom.

The only person who would pause and give me any sort of consideration was my sister, Judy. She would always halt and ask if I wanted to join. She would regard me with pity in her eyes and concern in her voice. "Hey, just for this one night, come have a good time with us. I promise we won't do anything that would get you in trouble with mama. Just come along. All you do at night is read books. You must have read every book on planet earth by now. Just come along for this one night."

I would always smile when she said that. I knew she genuinely cared for me. My contentment was found within the pages of books, with black letters against white backgrounds. I had a passion for learning new words and marveled at how writers could mold and weave paragraphs with such ease. That was my place of peace, just as a party was her sanctuary. She could hardly finish her plea before my oldest brother would shout, "Come on, girl, we're going to be late. Don't worry about that boy; he's with his books. Leave him right there. Sooner or later, he'll fall into a stupor behind those books. Come on now, the party isn't going to wait for us."

With those admonishing words, my sister would wave at me with sorrow in her eyes and sprint off to catch up with my brothers.

In their minds, I suppose I was the odd one, the one who seemed distant and lacking in friends. Yet, my companions were my books. I often delved into tales of distant places or read about characters who appeared as if they stood right before me. Books transported me far from my New Orleans neighborhood, placing me out at sea or in realms of imagination. Books spoke to my soul, enabling me to break free from a certain type of mental confinement. My excitement knew no bounds when it came to acquiring new books. I would order volumes of short stories, novels, sports, world news, and works of fiction.

I found contentment on my front porch, just as I found contentment in letting my brothers and sisters head off to parties without me. And so, here I was once again, perched on the top step of the porch, reading under the glow of the streetlamp. My thirst to absorb words and knowledge was insatiable at times. If not for my mother's words of concern, I might find myself outside reading until one or two o'clock in the morning. I'd read to the backdrop of passing cars or the chorus of cicadas with their rhythmic clicking. Occasionally, I'd catch strains of music drifting from the barroom, making its way down the street. These were my nights, and my books were my solace.

Playground Paradise

There was a fine line that I walked as a child. The line that determined if I should listen to my parents or venture off into my own world. As a young kid, not even ten years old, I had a tendency to venture off. Venturing off was costly and I had to pay the consequences. I remember the time I ventured off in the grocery store and was separated from my mother. This was after her stern warning admonishing me not to wander off. Her words still ring in my memory now, "Stay close to me at all times. They take children like you."

I listened to her words and understood them, yet there was a wandering spirit about me. I would venture off and explore things out of curiosity or just plain stubbornness. I understood her instructions in the grocery store fully, yet it was something that grabbed my attention and I wandered off to investigate it. My grocery store venture not only ended with another stern warning, but it came with a powerful swat on my behind and a reinforcement of her words. "Didn't I tell you to stay close to me? Now wander off again and see what happens. Don't test me boy."

You would think that with such an admonishment, enforced through a forceful swat on my behind, I would have learned my lesson. If only life were that simple and free of complications. It wasn't too long after that incident that my mother was walking with me to the corner store so I could get a frozen cup—a New Orleans treat that I so looked forward to. All I had to do to earn my allowance was to clean my room. Once that was accomplished, I would be rewarded with a quarter, and that was the cost of a frozen cup.

We made it to the corner store, where I would usually see the other kids from the neighborhood. However, today was different.

There were no kids, and even my mother noticed the difference. She inquired of the storekeeper, "It doesn't seem busy today. That is odd on a hot summer day. I'm used to your place being packed with kids."

The storekeeper responded, "Well, they will be in here in about an hour. They just opened that new playground across N. Prieur Street, before you get to Laharpe Street. Everything in it is brand new. They have a new merry-go-round, swing sets, sliding boards, and monkey bars. Those kids will be in here after they wear themselves out, plus it is hot too. Oh yeah, it is just a matter of time before they flood this place."

My mother didn't say much as we walked back home. It wasn't until we got home and she was wiping the red dye from the frozen cup off my face. "Son, I want to get one thing straight. That new park the storekeeper was talking about is across N. Prieur Street, and you know you're not allowed to cross that street. There is two-way traffic, and it is too dangerous. I know you can get caught up in your own mind sometimes and wander off, but you're not to go anywhere near that busy street. Do you understand?"

Before I could answer her, thoughts about that new playground filled my mind. I heard her words, but there were images in my mind of climbing the ladder of the sliding board and swinging on the swing sets. With a timid voice, I answered my mother, "Yes, I understand." I remember her smile as she said, "Okay, now go wash your hands and get ready for dinner."

If only the story ended there, with no fanfare, but it didn't. For the next few days, I watched all the kids from the neighborhood venture down to N. Prieur Street and carefully cross the busy street heading to the new park. I felt lonely because I was the only kid who could not go. I felt like I was missing out on the adventure of a lifetime. My mother would sometimes sit on the front porch and watch me play. She spoke to me as if she was reading my mind. "Don't worry, those kids will be back in a little while. I can't imagine how their parents allow them to cross that busy street by themselves. One of those kids is going to get hurt. Those cars on N. Prieur Street drive so fast and they are not looking out for children."

I heard her words and remembered her instructions, but that thing inside of me that makes me venture off was speaking to me. It was telling me that if I was careful and looked both ways, I could cross that busy street. That I could make it across N. Prieur Street and into that park, where all the kids were having such a good time.

It only took a few more days until I was convinced that I could do it. I figured in my mind that if my mother ever found out, she would be proud of me for crossing the street like an older kid would do. I had made up my mind that today was the day of venturing off. I waited until my mother started cooking in the kitchen. I could see her through the window. I knew she wouldn't be on the front porch for a while because she was tending to the pots on the stove.

So I started walking down the street. My feet were moving at an unusually fast pace, and I was nervous. I knew I was going against her wishes, but something about the lure of that park was calling me. As I approached N. Prieur Street, I decided to stop and look both ways. I placed my hand on the bumper of a parked car and looked around the front hood. I looked both ways, and to my delight, there was no moving traffic. I checked one more time and then darted across the street to safety.

Still nervous, I made my way to the park. As I entered the park, I could see all the children from my neighborhood. They were all playing on the merry-go-round and the swings. They were filled with happiness, and the expressions on their faces showed pure joy. What could be better for a kid than playing in the park? I joined in with the other kids, and we played for what seemed like an eternity. No one was tired, and no one cared about anything else not even frozen cups.

One of the mothers from the neighborhood was there, and she asked me, "Does your mother know you're here? I know your mother, and she would have a fit if she knew you were here without her." I quickly turned to her and lied, "Yes, she knows."

The lady gave me a look that indicated she didn't believe me, but it didn't matter. All that was on my mind was having fun. We all continued to play, and I decided I wanted to try out the slide. The other kids were laughing and saying that the slide was hot from the summer heat and that you had to slide down quickly, or you would burn your legs. All the kids were sliding down as fast as possible to avoid burning their legs on the hot metal of the slide. I got in line to take my turn. I climbed the metal steps to the top of the slide. As I reached the top step and looked over, to my surprise and shock, my mother was at the bottom of the slide.

She had a look of pure anger and indignation on her face. Before she could say a word, I nervously made my way down the steps of the slide. She had that leather belt in her hand, and I knew what that meant. I wanted nothing to do with it. I took off running back toward home. I turned momentarily to see my mother running at full speed. I had no idea she knew how to run; she wasn't a kid, so how did she know how to run?

I ran as fast as I could, and as I approached N. Prieur Street, I didn't take time to stop and look both ways like I did earlier. I just darted across the street, and to my shock, there was a car coming at full speed. The driver must have seen me and slammed on his brakes, causing his tires to screech and the car to slide to one side. In my brief state of shock, I froze and covered my ears. I could hear the scream coming from my mother. She was in just as much shock and awe as I was. I gathered myself and hid behind a parked car. I listened as she called out my name with fear and panic in her voice. I remained hidden behind that car. I could hear her panicked voice calling my name. As she got closer, once again, I took off running. I could hear her yell out, "Don't you run from me, boy. Just wait until you get home!"

There's really no need to go into further detail about what

happened when she finally returned home. I think, as any Black person, we can all imagine the outcome. I wasn't sure why I had the tendency to overlook my mother's cautioning. Maybe it was the voice that steered me away from her in the grocery store. Perhaps I was just a curious kid who couldn't resist his need for adventure. Either way, I never ventured into that park again. I even imagined a scenario where my mother and I would walk hand in hand, safely crossing N. Prieur Street together. I had visions of playing on the playground until I was simply worn out. But that was just a dream. I learned my lesson and paid the price for my disobedience. At least I was still alive to tell the story.

Wit's End

"Take him! I said, 'Take him, dammit, and get him the hell out of my house!'" Those were the words that came out of my mother's mouth as the police hauled me away, like the trash man hauling off trash you leave out on garbage day. Yet that was my last hope, and she turned her back on me and let them take me.

I would be lying to you if I said I wasn't a troubled child. I managed to get myself into trouble from the time I could walk and talk. It didn't take long for me to find trouble, or should I say, trouble found me. I actually have no excuse other than it makes me feel good. Getting in trouble actually brings a smile to my face, but not this time. This time it is serious because my mother has never turned me in. She has lied for me, stolen for me, worked two jobs for me, lost a husband because of me, and lost the trust of friends and family behind me.

My father left us because my mother would not allow him to raise me the right way. My father was a straight-laced guy who wore a shirt and tie every day, and his shoes shined like bright new pennies. The men on the block called it a spit shine. As a child, I would go with him to get those shoes shined, and I would jump every time the shine man popped the rag. My father would not leave the shoe shine man until he could see his reflection in those shoes. He would pay the man and then slide him a tip to reward the extra shine. I remember those days so vividly, and it inspired me to be so different. I didn't hate my father, but I knew I could never be like him. I was so comfortable in blue jeans, V-neck t-shirts, and low-top tennis shoes.

I would go down to Canal Street and scope out the stores with lazy salesmen. The guys who would rather watch people promenade down the street instead of keeping an eye on their inventory. I would take any opportunity to pounce and walk right out of the front door with merchandise that I did not pay for. When I got home, my father would question me about my new tennis shoes or my new blue jeans. Before I could make up a lie, my mother would be right there to defend me. She would put her hands on her hips and give my father the meanest looks. With venom in her voice, she would say, 'Vernell, why are you bothering that boy? Leave him alone! He does odd jobs around the neighborhood and cuts grass to earn the money to buy nice things. Do you really think you're the only person in this family who has a right to look good?'

My father would back down from his interrogation and give in to my mother's loud rantings. He was a kind man, and I took advantage of his weakness for peace. He was not a man to argue, and he especially didn't like to argue with my mother. Once she started to raise her voice, I knew he would back down and go back to reading his newspaper. I would refer to him as Church Boy when he wasn't around.

My mother was that type of person who always looked out for me. I guess that is why I am so puzzled about why she let the police take me this time. I know everything and everyone has a limit, but 'damn,' Mama, do you really have any idea where they are taking me? It is a Friday night, and I know I will have to sit in jail until I can see a judge on Monday. Does she know that she is setting me up for a horrible weekend in jail, or is it that she doesn't care anymore?"

As the cops place me in the back of the car, I turn my head to take a glance at my mother. I'm hoping that she will change her mind and ask the cops to release me. I turn and give her the saddest, guilt-driven look I can muster, but she doesn't budge. I feel a tear start to well up in the corner of my eye, but I can't wipe it away because I'm cuffed. Just as the darkness of my life starts to cave in on me, I turn to see my mother racing toward the police car. She yells at the police to stop and beckons one of the officers out of the car. I start to feel that naughty feeling again, and that devious smile starts to come to my face. Here's my saving grace once again coming to my aid. I know it will be a matter of minutes before the cops release me from these cuffs and let me go. I don't care how much she'll fuss at me or how hard she'll pop me in the back of the head, all I want is out of the backseat of this cruiser.

The cop finishes talking to my mother and makes his way over to the back door of the car. I know this is the time to receive my freedom, and I can't hide that devilish smile no matter how hard I try. The cop opens the back door to the cruiser and allows my mother to stick her head in. With a blank stare, she looks me in the eyes and growls, "Boy, get that stupid look off your face. Every fiber of my being wants you to be free and out of those cuffs, but I know you'll simply do the same thing again. I'm tired. I'm tired of sacrificing for you, and in return, I get no positive results. I have lost so much trying to keep you out of prison, but you repay me with more pain. I wanted to take the time to tell you not to bring yourself around my house ever again. You're of age, and I am not putting up with this for another minute of my life. I am tired of wondering where you are and what you're up to. Today is my final day of living like this!"

With those words, she slams the door to the cruiser, and I know she's serious. I know I'm on my own, and I have no one to blame but myself. I had gotten a sick thrill out of stealing, robbing, and committing all sorts of stupid crimes, and now it's time to pay the piper."

Choices

I can always tell when winter is on the horizon; it takes me longer to get going in the morning, mostly because of this bad knee of mine – the result of a gunshot wound I sustained as a teenager. I came from a loving, church-going family, yet I was one of those kids filled with mischief. I could never sit down and listen to sermons at church, so I would fidget the entire time.

I couldn't keep my focus on schoolwork. When the teacher was speaking, I was that kid who would make airplanes out of sheets of paper and gaze out of the window. The only subject I really enjoyed was math, partly because it came easy to me. There was something about numbers that never presented a challenge; I had a knack for them, and my teachers would always encourage me to stand out in math class. I thought standing out is for suckers. That was my mindset, even if I didn't voice those sentiments until I felt I was old enough – that age when calling my parents didn't matter anymore.

I began to find fulfillment in childish nonsense, such as pulling on car door handles to see if someone had left their car unlocked. If they were foolish enough to do so, then I was daring enough to take whatever I thought was valuable. It all started there and progressed to putting bags of chips under my sweater and candy treats in my pockets. The corner store clerk became all too aware of my childish misdeeds and eventually banned me from the store.

I had a couple of run-ins with the police. On one occasion, I was on Olga Street and impulsively stole a kid's bicycle. I didn't really need or want a bicycle, but I did it for the thrill of mischief. The police found me three blocks away after I had abandoned the bicycle on the ground – I couldn't even manage to ride of it for three blocks without getting tired.

This was the first time my parents had to come see me at the police station, and unfortunately, it wouldn't be the last. I spent my teenage years in and out of trouble. Finally, it all came to an end on a cold winter evening, much like today.

There was an old man who lived around the corner on Ida Street. Rumors circulated throughout the neighborhood that he was wealthy and kept substantial amounts of cash in his house. It was said that he stored socks filled with old coins in his bedroom dresser drawers. For someone like me, prone to mischief and curiosity, this was an irresistible temptation. I often saw the old man walking to the store on cool fall afternoons, so I hatched a plan to break into his home the next time he headed to the store.

Several weeks later, news circulated that the old man was sick and needed someone to deliver groceries to his house. Seizing the opportunity, I approached the store clerk and offered to do the task in exchange for a small fee. It wasn't an act of kindness; rather, I had a cunning plan. My intention was to gain entry into the house, distract the old man, and keep him occupied in the kitchen. This would give me the chance to rush to one of his dresser drawers, grab a sock filled with old coins, and make a swift exit.

The store clerk agreed to let me take the bags of groceries, but not without a final warning as I exited through the glass door. "No foolishness from you. I've never known you to do something nice for someone, but I need those groceries to reach that old man. I'll pay you when you return to the store, and only if I'm convinced he received his groceries."

With those words in mind, I proceeded down the block toward the old man's house. I carefully ascended the steps to his front porch, ensuring the brown grocery bags remained intact. Just as I was about to knock on the screen door, the wooden door swung open, revealing an elderly gentleman who welcomed me inside. He remarked, "I've never seen you before. Are you new to the job? If you're going to be my regular guy, just know that I'll be expecting a delivery from you once a week from now on. I've been suffering with the flu, and it's becoming increasingly difficult for me to walk to the store. If you don't mind, could you place those bags in the kitchen?"

His house was a typical New Orleans shotgun double. To reach the kitchen, located at the very back of his house, I had to pass by his bedroom. As I walked by, I discreetly noted the location of the dresser. My plan was to divert his attention and then stealthily move my way to the dresser drawers. I intended to grab whatever valuables I could find and then make a hasty exit.

As I reached the kitchen, the old man engaged me in conversation. Seizing the moment, I called out, "Hey, you might want to come into the kitchen and take a look at this carton of eggs. Let's make sure none of them are broken. If any are, I'll gladly return the carton and get you a fresh one."

My intention was to use this distraction as a cover while I executed my plan in his bedroom.

The old man made his way into the kitchen and I slid pass him just like a snake would slitter in the grass. I hurried and ran to the dresser and opened the top drawer. I noticed his socks but when I got ready to grab them and run, I noticed that they were lightweight. There was no coins in these socks, they were just socks. Before I could close the drawers the old man was in the doorway of the bedroom looking at me.

"What in the world are you doing" he belted out in an aggravated voice. I panicked and started running toward the front door, but before I could make my escape I heard a loud pop. It startled me and I momentarily froze in my tracks.

But I couldn't just stop, I had to get out of his house because that pop that I heard was a shot from his gun. Before I could gather myself to keep running, I heard another pop and I felt a burn on the back of my leg. The adrenalin was racing through my body, the fact that I was shot didn't stop me from running. I made my way home and my parents rushed me to the hospital.

It was from there that I ended up in juvenile corrections. I spent a total of three years there, locked up like an animal. Yet, I could not blame anyone but myself. It was my doing and my choice. While in corrections, I was offered to take a course on basic bookkeeping and some advanced math. Numbers were never a challenge for me but this kept my mind occupied.

That was many years ago. I am a grown man now, but the lingering effects of that gunshot still haunt me to this day. I don't need to consult the weather forecast to know when the seasons are changing – my knee serves as a reliable barometer. I utilized that bookkeeping program to secure a real job, and I've been steadily employed for years now. As I get ready to leave for work, bracing for the cool fall day, my attention is drawn to the reflection of red and blue lights bouncing off my walls. Those colored lights are all too familiar to me.

I approach the front window, parting the blinds to get a glimpse of the situation outside. Several of my neighbors are on their porches, observing as the police restrain a teenage boy. They press him against a car and conduct a thorough search of his pockets. I recognize that look on his face – a mixture of mischief and a slight, knowing smile. It's as if this moment is his chance to gain some form of attention that may be missing in his life. Perhaps, he's fueled by the same curiosity and mischief that once consumed me. I understand his pain and feel his desperation. My wish is for someone to extend compassion to him and offer a program that can shape his future.

I finish my last sip of coffee, adjust my hat on my head, and begin my journey out of the house, heading toward another day of honest and legitimate work. My hope extends to that young man and the potential for a brighter future for him.

It's Over

My grandpa would always say, "It is better to love and experience loss than to never experience either one." I didn't think too much of his words until today, now that my heart is broken. Love hurts more than a root canal, and I've had a few root canals in my life.

I first laid eyes on her as she sat alone at a table, engrossed in her physics book. I frequented this coffee shop on Esplanade Avenue hidden among the mighty oak trees. I lived in the area, and the manager of the coffee shop is my neighbor, so I stopped by at least once a week to chit-chat a bit. Despite my frequent visits, I had never seen this woman before, or anyone as beautiful as she was. I was stunned by her beauty and paralyzed to the point that I couldn't imagine approaching her. I asked my neighbor, if he knew her name, but he shook his head to signal a negative response. He mentioned that she always paid with cash.

I found myself at a crossroads, faced with the decision to either approach this beautiful woman or forever lose the opportunity to know her. Finally, I managed to get my knees to cooperate with my heart, and I made my way toward her table. However, before I could open my mouth and speak as smoothly as a poem, she reached for her tray with trash on it and handed it to me. So, I did what any self-respecting man would do and took her tray over to the trash can, dumping the trash. I laughed the entire time on the way to the trash can. As I turned back toward her table, she was gone. My neighbor pointed toward the back door, and I hurriedly followed her outside. I was able to get her attention before she reached her car, and with all the courage I could muster, I spoke the following words: "You know it's not polite to stiff the busboy."

She smiled and reached into her purse to get me a tip, but I reached over and touched her hand, stopping her. She looked at me with a quizzical expression and asked if I wanted a tip or not. I told her that the coffee shop had no busboys, and I was headed to her table to introduce myself to her. Once again, she smiled, and this time she extended her hand to shake mine. That's how our relationship started—a moment straight out of a movie, or the kind of scene you'd see in a Saturday afternoon play.

We remained in the parking lot and talked for almost an hour, utterly smitten with each other. We exchanged phone numbers, and from that day on, we were an inseparable part of each other's lives. Our relationship was the stuff of love songs, the kind of love you hear women sing about. We would spend time at each other's apartments, doing all the things lovers do. We went to Mardi gras parades together, and I cherished the moments when she would climb onto my shoulders to catch beads from passing floats.

We cooked for one another, and on the days she needed time to study, those were the hardest days to endure. I would pace the floor of my apartment, anxiously waiting for the phone to ring, longing to hear her voice tell me she was finished studying for the night. It's crazy how someone can have such an influence over your daily life. We planned our evenings around Black cinema and jazz CDs. We explored the New Orleans nightlife, discovering jazz clubs and late-night food spots. We acted like tourists in our own town, laughing at the comedians who performed between jazz sets while the musicians changed outfits. We later admitted that our days felt incomplete without each other, and we eagerly awaited the end of our day's activities just to be together again. We disagreed on what constituted good television and took long walks that always seemed to lead us to elderly trees of City Park.

It was love, and for the first time in my life, I wanted it to last forever, with no end in sight. I had visions of the house we would buy, our kids racing through the streets, knocking over garbage cans as they learned to skate. I thought of a wedding and how I wanted both of our families to get along seamlessly, like a perfectly woven cloth. We had a perfect love affair until an event came along to shatter my dreams—an event that is usually celebrated with happiness: graduation. It never occurred to me that all her studying and test-taking would ultimately lead to this conclusion. I viewed college as a period of unbearable separation from each other, nothing more, and nothing less. I never asked her about her dreams or aspirations because I had my own vision of a Mid-City house, kids skating in the street, harmonious family gatherings, and a life happily ever after. I never thought enough about her to inquire about her visions for her future or our future together. Maybe I was afraid that her vision would differ from mine and somehow wouldn't include me. I feared that if her vision didn't include me, I wouldn't be able to convince her to change her mind and reconsider us. So I remained silent, enjoying the bliss of our relationship as we met under warm covers and watched as actors play different roles in movies.

One day, everything changed as she excitedly packed up brown boxes with packing tape and markers to identify each one. As I entered her apartment, she was almost finished with her packing, and her once cozy apartment was now filled with boxes and packing tape. She seemed unfazed, as if nothing was wrong and nothing was about to change. However, my heart sank deeper and deeper into my chest.

It felt like a scene from a movie where the guy walks in and finds his girl in bed with another lover. In this case, her packed boxes were the other lover, and its name was "Moving On." I mustered the courage to ask her if she had ever planned on discussing her plans with me, given that we were in love. She calmly continued packing clothes, glancing at me, and uttered those words that shattered my heart even further, "Were we really in love, or were we just having a good time together?"

My heart now felt like it was on the floor, and she didn't step around it but right on it. I tried to explain how deeply in love I was with her, how I had already picked out a house, envisioned our future with kids, and the perfect relationship for our families. I was hoping for a response that would salvage our love, but all she did was smile at me, giving me a sympathetic hug, and gently stroke my face.

At that moment, I thought she would give me a speech about her fear of commitment but a willingness to try love with me. Instead, she tilted her head slightly and began telling me about a job offer she had received out of town. She confessed that she hadn't told me earlier because she could see that I was in love with her, but she didn't share those same feelings. She appreciated the movies, the late nights under warm blankets, the parades, the late-night jazz clubs, and of course, the intimacy we had shared. But she made it clear that she wasn't ready for a husband because her career was her primary focus.

Despite the overwhelming urge to break down and cry, I held my composure and simply walked out of her apartment. I left with a heart full of pain, a wounded soul, and the echoing words of my grandpa in my ear. I had experienced love and the accompanying heartache, but his words were not the ones I wanted to hear in that moment.

Four Walls, Five Years

There was a saying I once heard about how to make a person lose their mind. It spoke about loneliness and how isolation can impact the mind. I'm not sure of the exact quote or who said it, but I can attest to the fact that loneliness is a weapon and can be more destructive than a bomb.

I have been long removed from what people call normal society. I am serving a twenty-five-year sentence on multiple drug charges, ranging from possession to distribution to traveling over state lines. I have already served the majority of my time, with five more years to go. While I have not been alone all the time, as I have the company of my fellow inmates, they are a constant reminder of the life I left behind. The constant bickering and the feeling that everything is being bartered as if we were living in the Wild West. Despite the occasional fights and threats of violence, I cherish my fellow inmates in a strange way. They serve as a reminder of the life I never want to live again. I try to keep my bartering to a minimum, focusing only on the items I really need.

I have learned to live by my needs and to suppress my wants. Giving in to my wants is part of the reason I am in this prison now.

Have you ever met a guy who just overwhelms your senses? That is how I felt when I met Lawrence. We lived on the same street, and all we really shared in common was the neighborhood. We attended the same schools and frequented the same house parties, but Lawrence wasn't impressed by me. Maybe it was because of the age difference, or maybe it was because he never found me attractive. Yet, all that changed one night at a house party. I was having a typical night, occasionally dancing but never to a slow record. I had a beer that I held on to for dear life, simply because I wasn't really into alcohol. I did have one vice that Lawrence and I shared, and that was cigarettes.

I stepped outside to smoke a cigarette, and there he was. He was just cool. He wasn't the smart kid or the athlete; he had a style of his own and a confident quietness about him. We struck up an awkward conversation that turned into an hour-long conversation. I had a major crush on him, but he had other plans in mind. We exchanged phone numbers, and the next week, we spent every moment we could muster talking on the phone. My conversation stemmed from a schoolgirl crush, but his conversation seemed to be more like an interview than anything else.

To cut to the chase, Lawrence was a drug dealer, and I would turn out to be his runner. I would do anything for him, and in reality, I did just about anything for him. I compromised my body, mind, and freedom for Lawrence. I've had years to get him out of my system, as I have yet to hear from him. All these years in prison, and not a peep from him. I guess it really was a one-way street of infatuation.

That was so many years ago, and I am reminded of my bad decisions every day. I wake to the sound of arguing women, the barks of officers, and the glimmer of sunshine that shines through the window.

There was a miracle that occurred in my life a few years ago. I entered another inmate's cell to get my hair braided, and I noticed that she had a book partially hidden under her covers. What drew my attention was the colorful cover of the book. It was bright yellow, and for some reason, the color represented life and joy. Life and joy are two things that are not readily available in prison. I reached for the book, just to see if I could see the entire cover, and right at that moment, my hand was slapped, and I was reprimanded by the other inmate.

"Don't ever put your hands on anything in my cell. That book has nothing to do with you and has nothing to do with getting your hair braided. Mind your business, mind your manners!"

I did what I was told and never mentioned it while I was getting my hair braided, but the curiosity was killing me. As I got ready to leave, I looked at the bedspread once again, to see the outline of the book. Finally, the other inmate said, "That book is really driving you crazy. If you want, I can loan it to you, but you have to keep it private or the guards will take it. Do not mention it to the others on the cell block because I don't want anyone to know that I am an avid reader. Go ahead, take it. If you enjoy it, then I will share another one with you."

I was uncertain at first. I didn't know if she was sincere or if this was another bartering angle. Yet, the book was driving my curiosity, and the yellow colors on the cover were actually calling me. I hurried and placed the book under my shirt and scurried off to my cell. The other inmate gave me a warm smile and some final words of caution. "I usually read around three o'clock in the morning. I guess in my former life, I was so used to getting up for work at three o'clock that my body just knows when to get up. There should be a ray of life from the outside that beams through your window. Use that light to illuminate the pages and just get lost in the context of the book. Let your mind send you to the places the book speaks of and let yourself become the characters. Hell, we don't have anything else to do around here so why not."

With her words secured in my mind, I ventured off to my cell and hid the book. The first two nights I slept right past the three o'clock hour, and when I finally woke up, it was always time for breakfast, and the light of day was shining bright. Yet, the book stayed on my mind, and eventually, I began to wake up in the early hours of the morning to read.

The other inmate was right in her admonition. I did find myself getting lost in the characters and allowing my mind to think of the places that were outlined in the book. It was like a drug to me, at least it gave me that same yearning as I had for drugs. I read through the first book and asked if I could keep it to read it again. I was surprised because I was never the studious type, and I never had any passion for reading. I guess being locked up can change your passions.

The other inmate and I would occasionally meet and discuss the last books we had read. She confided in me that she was in prison for stealing money from the company that she worked for. She stated that it wasn't just a little money, but she had bilked the company out of thousands of dollars before she was caught. She came across as a really smart woman, and she finally let me know how she was getting so many books.

She confided in me that she was a twin, and her twin sister would send her a book once every other month. She told me that she and her sister share an unbreakable bond that even the walls of prison can't destroy. Her sister would shop for books at a neighborhood bookstore located on Bayou Road in New Orleans. She stated that her sister knew what types of books she liked and she would send at least one book every other month. One month it would be a book of fiction, then one on short stories, and then one on a murder mystery. She also shared that if I wanted, she could write her sister and tell her to send two books, and I could have one.

Since her offer, which I accepted, I have been biding my time with my head buried in a book. The other inmate and I will share our thoughts on the different books, all the while keeping our interest from the other inmates and the guards. Living in an environment like this teaches you that something as innocent as a shared love of books can be held against you.

So, I read and I allow my mind to take me to far-off places and to put me in unbelievable situations. The loneliness of prison can be overcome, and I found my way to overcome it. I find myself lost in the pages of books that I would have never paid attention to in my past life.

Franklin

I would scale tall mountains and walk across alligator-infested waters for my son because I love that boy. My wife and I struggled to start a family, but when she was pregnant with my son, I had a feeling he would be special, and he is. I know most fathers think their kid is special, but this little guy is my heart and soul. We share a bond that I would have never imagined.

From an early age, he showed an intense interest in basketball. As a toddler, he would stand in front of the television as if he were in a trance. I had always imagined that I would be his hero, but I had been replaced by a basketball player.

My son had an undying fascination with Franklin. Now, you can recognize a star player when they only go by one name. That was Franklin. His poster hung on my son's bedroom wall, and I paid a few hundred dollars for his tennis shoes. My son would go on endlessly about Franklin, even though most kids around eleven years old would be fascinated with other things. My son knew Franklin's birthday, where he went to high school, how he skipped going to college – he knew it all.

I had a surprise for my son that I had been keeping a secret. Franklin's team was coming to town, and I wanted to get tickets to the game. My son never mentioned going to the game; all he asked was that we watch the game together on the big television. I would do anything to make this kid happy, so I signed up for overtime at my job every day, seven days a week, to get good seats. I didn't want to sit at the top of the arena; I wanted the best seats that I could pay for. I wanted my son to have that up-close experience of seeing his hero.

I worked at a warehouse on Old Gentilly Road, and the guy who owned the business noticed my increase in hours. He stopped me and asked if everything was alright at home and if I was in need of money. I explained to him that I was working all the overtime I could to afford nice seats so my son could watch the world famous, Franklin play in person. The owner smiled and invited me into his office. Through a look of disappointment, he said, "I have been blessed in this life to have money, family, and my health. In the midst of building this life, I spoiled my kids to the point that they're now trash. They do drugs, buy expensive stuff that they never use, and they are lazy. I'm telling you this because a few years ago, I bought them courtside seats, season tickets, and not once have they gone to a game. I want to gift you with their two tickets and the parking pass. Go and enjoy the game with your son. I hope he never forgets how hard you work and how much you love him."

I can't begin to describe what this gift meant to me. Courtside seats are reserved for the rich or the famous, and I was neither. Yet for one night, I would be able to make my son's dream come to fruition. He would get an up-close view of his hero.

On the night of the game, we made our way to the arena. As I pulled up to the parking garage, the attendant waved me to the private section of parking. He opened my door and instructed me on where to find the elevator that would take us to the court-side seating. I could see the excitement on my son's face the entire time we were walking to our seats. He was amazed at how big the players were, but he didn't see his hero on the court. I asked the couple sitting next to us if they had seen Franklin warming up. The wife, while spilling her glass of wine, stated that Franklin only warmed up for a few minutes and then jogged to the locker room.

In my mind, I was hoping that Franklin would play because I didn't want anything to disappoint my boy. Sure enough, when the game started, there was Franklin. He was a larger-than-life figure to my son, and everything he did was larger than life to my son.

My son screamed his name the entire time Franklin was on the court, but Franklin ignored my son's cries. I will admit that it was starting to get to me a bit because I knew Franklin could hear him. One time, the team inbounded the basketball right in front of us. My son sat back in awe as if he had seen an angel up close and personal. Instead of screaming out his name, my son sunk in his seat and looked at me, and with a low tone in his voice said, "Dad, that's Franklin." I thought it would be the highlight of the night, but I was mistaken. As the final horn went off, and the game was finalized, we began to head to the exit.

My son was still in basketball heaven telling me every move that Franklin made and how he wore his socks and tied his shoes. Then out of the blue, I noticed Franklin running over to where we were standing. He yelled out, "Hey kid!" My son turned around and froze. Franklin smiled and said, "I heard you yelling my name all night. Thanks for the support."

I turned to see my son in a state of mid shock. All those years of hearing about Franklin and now he is speechless. Franklin took off his wrist bands and his headband and gave it to my son. Just when I thought it couldn't get any better, Franklin looked at me and said, "Is it okay if we take a picture together?"

I gave my phone to the couple who sat next to us and they snapped pictures of me, my son and Franklin on the court. My son was in hog heaven. I had never seen a kid smile so wide. When the pictures were taken, Franklin shook my son's hand and said, "Thank you."

The moment was perfect as was the night. I cannot began to describe the feeling of fulfilling a kid's dream. I hope he grows up to be another Franklin or even a man who loves his kids and would climb mountains and walk across alligator infested waters for them.

Saturday Afternoon

The heat was blistering that day, typical of New Orleans where even winter days felt like summer's dog days. This year seemed particularly hot for some reason. With summer programs gone and the neighborhood pool drained, there wasn't much for a kid like me to do. So, I wandered the streets, hoping to find something to occupy my mind.

Suddenly, I spotted him standing on the corner, a beer in hand, chatting with his friends. "Daddy! Hey, daddy!" I yelled, but my voice seemed too weak for him to hear over the street noise. I sprinted towards him, trying to reach him before he disappeared back into the barroom.

Children weren't allowed in the barroom, or else the city would fine them.

As I approached, he raised his head and recognized me. With a disheveled look, he called out, "June bug, why are you running so fast? Where are you going, boy?" I caught my breath and gathered my thoughts before responding, "Daddy, I miss you. Why are you drinking a beer in the afternoon?"

His friends chuckled, one of them mocking me by echoing my words. Unfazed by their laughter, my father knelt down to straighten my shirt and said, "June bug, I've got a surprise for you. Check out what's in the top pocket of my shirt." Sure enough, there were football tickets for tomorrow's college game. Overcome with excitement, I hugged him tightly.

He leaned back slightly and continued, "Meet me by the big gate at the front of the stadium. I would come and get you from the house, but I don't want to deal with your mama's nagging. She'd be asking when I'll bring you back and where I got the tickets. That's why I left that house; too much nosiness for my liking. Can't stand a nagging, nosy woman. It's a terrible combination."

At that moment, his words blurred together because all I could focus on was the fact that we were going to the football game tomorrow. The stadium was right in the heart of Uptown New Orleans, just blocks from our house, yet a place I had never set foot in before.

My father loved football, always glued to the TV during games. But by halftime, he'd often be passed out from one too many beers. I'd cheer and yell at the screen with all my might, but his slumber was more like a deep coma.

When Saturday arrived, I woke up early and dashed towards the stadium. By eleven o'clock, I was there, brimming with excitement and hope. It was my first football game, and I couldn't wait to experience it. But alongside my excitement, there lingered a hope that my father would show up. I desperately hoped he wasn't at home consumed by a bottle of beer, slipping towards unconsciousness.

Where was he? How long would I have to wait? Would this day, like so many others, end in disappointment? All through my school events and awards, he had been absent. It often seemed he preferred the company of the barroom to being around me. Noon approached, and the crowd started flowing into the stadium. I stood outside the gate where he was supposed to meet me, feeling a deep sense of loneliness. My hope began to dwindle, and shame crept in as I hung my head low.

I watched as other kids entered the gate with their fathers—some holding hands, others clutching programs or footballs. Despite my sinking heart, a smile flickered across my face as I yearned to trade places with them.

I longed to be that kid, experiencing the joy of a father's presence, holding hands, buying me a program and popcorn. But he wasn't there. As time ticked on and the area around the stadium emptied, the loudspeaker announced the starting players. It was shaping up to be another disappointment, another addition to the series of letdowns that seemed to define my young life.

Finally, I resigned myself to the truth like a child trying to grow up too soon. He wasn't coming. I kicked an empty can and turned to begin the lonely walk back home. I could hear the crowd starting to rumble from inside the stadium. This time, though, I refused to cry. It was time to accept him for who he was and stop yearning for who I wanted him to be.

Just as I started to walk away, a winded voice called out, "June bug, where are you going? The game has started, and I'm running late."

To be honest, I had never seen my father run before, but there he was, sprinting towards me with surprising speed. His paperboy cap flew off in the rush, causing him to pause briefly to retrieve it before continuing towards me. Catching his breath, he exclaimed, "June bug, come on, turn around! Let's get inside the stadium and find our seats. I'm sorry I'm late, son, but I stopped by the vendor to get you a program. Maybe we can get you a couple of autographs after the game."

With those words, I turned and walked alongside my father towards the grand gate. A man awaited, his arm outstretched to receive the tickets. My father reached into his shirt pocket and handed over two tickets. The man tore them in half and ushered us inside the stadium, a place I had only ever seen on TV. I paused, taking in the moment, and glanced at my father, who seemed just as thrilled as I was. If only every moment in my life could be like this Saturday afternoon.

Lover Girl

It's a three-hour drive back to New Orleans, and my boyfriend, Fred, hasn't spoken a word. I've tried to engage him in conversation, even asking several times if he wanted to stop for a bite to eat, but he hasn't responded. Not a single word, not even an utterance—just silence. Instead of pushing the issue, I've decided to look out the passenger window, watching the lush landscape pass by.

This silence began a few hours ago, at my college class reunion. It marked the tenth year since my graduation, and I had been looking forward to being back on campus. I was especially excited to see my sorority sisters. We had been so close and shared such good times. In my mind, those days seemed perfect, viewed through rose-colored glasses. I had almost forgotten the jealousy, backbiting, and cattiness that had simmered beneath the surface.

That jealousy reappeared the moment I was back with my sisters. I knew bringing Fred might stir things up, but I wanted them to see the man I love. I attended a small, private, all-girls liberal arts college, while Fred graduated from an HBCU. When he first told me about attending an HBCU, I must admit, I had no idea what it meant. I didn't know that Black people had to create their own schools because they were denied education and not allowed to attend most colleges. I've learned so much during my time with Fred.

I never really explained Fred to my sorority sisters. All they knew was that I had met a wonderful guy and that I was in love. They had no idea he was Black, and I never thought to mention it. Back in college, dating outside of our race was practically unheard of, but times have changed—it's been ten years. I knew some of them would be surprised, but I also knew which of my sisters I could trust to have my best interests at heart.

Remember the backbiting I mentioned earlier? My sorority sister, Penny, seemed especially taken with Fred. She went out of her way to make sure he had something to eat, and of course, something to drink. Then, she started interrogating him—asking how we met and whether our families were okay with the relationship. It was awkward, and I did my best to steer Fred away from her, trying to introduce him to other sisters. But Penny kept popping up, always with more questions.

Then, like a scene from a horror movie, Penny turned to Fred and asked, "Fred, do you know what her nickname was in college?" I felt my face flush red because my college nickname was "Lover Girl"—and not in an innocent way. When Fred heard it, he chuckled and gave me a playful look, as if he suddenly saw me as some naughty girl.

I thought I had dodged a bullet, as Fred didn't seem upset. But Penny wasn't finished. She went on to explain *why* I had earned that nickname. "Fred," she began, "there's an all-boys liberal arts college about a mile from ours. We used to go there on weekends and pick out boys—whether to date or have a fling with. Your honey wasn't much of a dater though. She preferred flings because she didn't want to be tied down. She wanted to sow her wild oats during her college years."

At this point, I could see Fred's demeanor shift. The playful, naughty-girl look he had given me moments earlier transformed into one of confusion and hurt, as if he no longer recognized me or the life I had lived. Penny continued to lay everything out in front of my sorority sisters, some of whom were raising their drinks to hide their shocked expressions. Others laughed, almost as if they had been waiting for this moment for years. Penny went on to name and describe the boys I had been involved with, as though she had been keeping a diary of my life.

It was humiliating—not because I regretted my college years, but because Fred was being dragged into this mess by women who were clearly trying to hurt me, and he didn't deserve any of it.

By the time Penny finished her little exposé, Fred's expression was one of pain. He looked at me as if he didn't know who I was anymore. I pulled him outside to the courtyard to talk, and things quickly became heated—something that surprised me because Fred is normally the most laid-back guy I've ever met.

I started by apologizing for Penny's behavior, assuring Fred that she was only doing this to embarrass me. Fred, however, asked if I had anything to say about what Penny had revealed. I firmly said, "No," because it was all true. I wasn't ashamed of my past. Yes, I had been adventurous in my love life during those years, but I didn't regret it. I met some interesting guys, shared intimate moments with them, and moved on. That was how I navigated life back then, but it's not how I live now—and it's definitely not how I treat Fred. I love him, and I would never be so cavalier about our relationship.

Unfortunately, my words did little to comfort Fred. He was silent, which was unusual for him, as he's typically a great communicator. His jaw was clenched, and I could see a vein pulsing on his forehead. I tried again, reminding him that this was ten years ago, during my college days. In an attempt to lighten the tension, I even asked if he could relate, thinking a good-looking guy like him must have had plenty of girlfriends in college.

When Fred finally spoke, he said, "I didn't date in college. I was too busy trying to get my degree while playing sports."

I playfully poked him in the ribs and teased, "Well, maybe you didn't have a girlfriend, but I know you must've hooked up from time to time."

Fred turned his back to me and mumbled, "No, I didn't. I had no hookups. I was focused on my religion, the discipline of sports, and graduating in four years. I had one girlfriend, but that was during my last semester, once I knew I'd graduate."

He then turned back to face me and said, "I didn't expect you to be a virgin when we met, but I also didn't expect you to have slept with most of the guys in western Louisiana."

With those words, I'd had enough. I snapped, "Fred, I'm not going to apologize to you for my college years, and I'm not going to make any excuses either. I did what I did, and I don't regret it. You weren't part of my life ten years ago, and you have no right to shame me for my past. You know I love you, and I would never step out on you if that's what you're worried about. While we're out here arguing, everyone inside is probably having a good laugh at this. I know this isn't funny to you, but Penny only said those things to hurt me and to use you against me. I want us to be together, but I'm not going to apologize for a life I lived ten years before meeting you!"

Fred pulled the car keys out of his pocket and said, "I'm going to sit in the car and try to clear my head. When you're ready to leave, that's where you'll find me, but I'm not going back into the party."

I begged Fred not to leave me alone at the party, knowing that his absence would only fuel Penny and the other messy girls. But he was resolute, so I went back inside, saying a few goodbyes to the sorority sisters who truly mattered to me. As I gathered my sweater and prepared to leave, I shot Penny an evil glare, making it clear that I wasn't backing down.

Sure enough, Fred was in the car, just as he said he'd be, shaking his head in frustration. I tried once more to console him and explain myself, but he didn't respond.

So, we started the three-hour drive back to New Orleans. A three-hour drive in silence.

Young Mr. Paul

Some things in life run like clockwork, and such was the case with Young Mr. Paul. Every Friday morning, long before the credit union opened, he would already be sitting on the steps, determined to be the first in line to deposit his money. The people of the Seventh Ward often said he was a go-getter.

Young Mr. Paul wasn't your average kid. He not only had a paper route in the mornings, but he also made a deal with the grocery store owner. The women in the neighborhood often found their grocery baskets too heavy to carry all the way home, so they'd wheel them as far as their houses and leave the baskets out front. Young Mr. Paul arranged to be paid a quarter for every basket he returned to the store.

Unlike most kids his age, Young Mr. Paul didn't have time for games of football on the patch of grass behind the library, nor did he shoot baskets at the hoop propped up against a telephone pole. He was entirely focused on making money, passing over the usual trappings of youth in pursuit of financial gain.

You see, Young Mr. Paul grew up in a house where money was often scarce. His father worked, but his mother did not, and there were times when it was hard to have everything they needed or wanted. He had his brother Joseph and his two sisters, Yvonne and Ronnie, to help look after, adding to the responsibility on his young shoulders.

As the clock inched closer to nine o'clock, Young Mr. Paul watched the tellers and loan officers approach the credit union. He greeted each of them by name as they climbed the three steps to unlock the door. In turn, they greeted him as if he were a member of their team, recognizing him not only for his presence but for his drive. They admired him, having never seen such an ambitious young man. One of the tellers even remarked, "Lord, I wish my husband worked as hard as this young man."

Today was Young Mr. Paul's lucky day. Not only did he have money to deposit, but he also had the opportunity to meet the President of the credit union. He was escorted down a long hallway to the President's office, where he was greeted by a stately man rising from behind a large desk. The man, dressed in a sharp blue suit with a matching bow tie, shook Young Mr. Paul's hand and led him into a nearby conference room.

The President introduced himself as Mr. Newman and began explaining how a credit union works and how it makes money. He told Young Mr. Paul that most of the credit union's earnings come from lending money to others. He gave an example: Young Mr. Paul's neighbor, wanting to build an addition to their home, didn't have the money upfront. So, they took out a loan from the credit union and paid it back with interest over time.

Young Mr. Paul was fascinated. He looked at Mr. Newman in awe and asked, "Sir, are you rich? Is that how you lend money to others? That's why I work so hard every day—so I can be rich like you and lend money, with interest, of course."

Mr. Newman chuckled and replied, "No, son, I'm not rich. The credit union pools money from people like you, and we lend it out. We take a bit of your money, and a bit of others' money, and then loan it out."

Young Mr. Paul's face grew serious, his brow furrowing in confusion. "Mr. Newman," he said, "I come here every Friday to deposit my money, and I think of your tellers as the people who protect it and make sure no one touches it. But now you're telling me you loan my money to other people?"

Mr. Newman chuckled and said, "Yes, that's how we survive in this business. We loan money and charge interest on it. That's how business works, son."

Hearing those unsettling words, Young Mr. Paul felt a surge of frustration. Without a word, he ran out of the conference room and headed straight home. His mind was racing, but he could still picture the old tin coffee cans scattered around the house—some filled with soil for his mother's green onions, one poked with holes and used as a heater in winter, and another filled with grease from frying his favorite speckled trout.

But Young Mr. Paul had a different idea. Without hesitation, he grabbed an empty coffee can with a plastic top from the cabinet and dashed out of the house, moving so quickly he skipped the back steps entirely.

With a single purpose in mind, he ran block after block until he found himself back at the credit union. Out of breath and with a sharp pain in his side, he burst through the glass doors and approached the teller's window, demanding all of his money.

The teller, recognizing him, looked surprised. "Young Mr. Paul, are you sure you want to withdraw all your money? This will close out your account. If you need money, why don't you have your parents come down and see about getting you a loan? We don't want to lose your business."

With a steadfast look on his face, Young Mr. Paul insisted that the teller give him every last dime in his account. The thought of his hard-earned money being loaned out to others filled him with anger and frustration. He was beside himself. He pulled out the coffee can and demanded that the teller put his money inside.

Afterward, Young Mr. Paul sprinted back home, thinking of ways to hide his money from his brother and sisters. He recalled the plumber who had worked on the pipes under their house last winter, and an idea struck him. His parents' house, like most in New Orleans' Seventh Ward, was raised off the ground, supported by cinder blocks. With the coffee can in hand, Young Mr. Paul crawled under the house until he reached the center. There, using his bare hands, he began to dig a hole in the ground. He dug until the coffee can fit perfectly, then covered it with dirt.

From that day on, once a week, Young Mr. Paul would crawl under the house to make his "deposit" into the coffee can. When one can was full, he'd secure another empty one and begin filling that. There was no more trust for the credit union, no more talk of loans or interest. Young Mr. Paul had found his own way to become rich—by digging up coffee cans filled with his hard-earned money.

Joel

I'm frustrated with Joel. He's never left his philandering ways behind. I knew he had a wandering eye when I met him, but I thought that would change once we got married. In the first few months of our marriage, I actually saw a minor difference in him. Usually, he's a very gregarious guy, with a flirtatious word for every woman he passes. Once we were married, I saw less and less of that behavior. He would tell me, "Baby, I don't mean any harm, it's just my personality. My daddy was like this too. A man of the people, always with a kind word even for strangers." That was his built-in excuse for flirting. I'll never forget the time we were at the French Market and he was looking at this woman a little too long. He walked away from me and over to her, and they started talking. I could actually see a twinkle in his eyes as they engaged in conversation. I tried not to show any weakness or signs of jealousy, but inside, I was burning up. Finally, he started walking toward me with this woman right by his side.

"Baby, I want you to meet Blake. From a distance, she looked like an old classmate of mine, but I was mistaken. I asked her to come over and meet you so she could share with you where she purchased her dress. I was telling her how beautiful her dress is and how it fits her figure just perfectly. I was wondering if you would buy your dresses from the same place and wear them for me."

I shook Blake's hand and tuned out anything and everything she was saying. I could see her mouth moving and her hands gesturing, but I was deaf to her words. Joel was standing there with a silly grin on his face, as if in some sort of state of euphoria. That was just one instance, and there were countless more, more than I want to recall right now.

I tried to turn the tide on him one day. We were at the bank, and

I walked away from Joel to approach the bank manager. He was a tall, handsome brother with an easy smile. I pulled him aside to engage in a meaningless conversation about checking accounts and dividends, but I made it seem like his every word made me laugh. When I turned to look at Joel, instead of being jealous and disrespected, he was engaged in conversation with the bank teller. There seemed to be no winning at this game of cat and mouse, but I refuse to feel insecure for the rest of my life, or at least the rest of this marriage.

My neighbor, Miss Alma, who shared the shotgun double house, used to sit on her porch and ask me, "Girl, do you know where your Joel is right now? It's damn near ten o'clock at night, and he hasn't shown up yet. That is a warning sign for a marriage. A man who can't make his way home after work is a man who has a woman on the other side of town. If I were you, I would confront him about it. Hell, I would even go inside and pack his bags and leave them on the sidewalk."

I had learned to tune out Miss Alma and her mess, but she was right. It was almost ten o'clock, and Joel had yet to show his face. I went inside and made sure that his food was warming in the oven. Just as I turned off the oven, I heard the key turning in the front door lock. There was Joel, with what used to be a dazzling smile, but now it was nothing but a silly childish grin, filled with mischief and devilment.

With my hands on my hips, I turned to Joel and asked him where he had been and why he was coming through the door so late. Joel couldn't look at me and hung his head, saying, "Baby, I was at the pool hall. A man who works as hard as I do deserves a cold beer after work and a game of nine ball. Don't you agree? I got carried away talking to the fellas, and before I knew it, time had slipped away from me."

I stopped Joel in the middle of his lie and said, "Joel, the pool hall has been closed for the last two weeks because they lost their liquor license (even though this was a lie, but I had to try and expose his lies). So how could you be in there if they're closed?"

Once again, Joel lowered his head and shied away from making eye contact with me. Suddenly, his demeanor changed, and he seemed to transform into another person. The gregarious guy turned into a demon. He said, "Look here, baby, I don't want to hurt your feelings, but you seem to ask for it. You know I wasn't playing pool, but what do you want me to say? Do you want me to say that I was at another woman's house, because that's where I was all this time? I try to keep my business out of your view, but when you insist on questioning me, I have no choice but to be honest with you. But this is your fault because you knew what type of guy I was when we started dating, and you knew how I was when we married. My wandering has as much to do with you and your choice of me as a husband as it does with me. So from this point forward, you can either accept me for who I am, or you can leave, but I know you're not leaving me. Now please pass me my plate of food because I am starving."

I must say, Joel never spoke so freely and openly as he just did. In a way, he was right; I knew how he was when we started dating. Hell, it was how we met. He approached me so smoothly and slyly, with an abundance of clever words and charm. Deep down inside, I knew he was incapable of being faithful to one woman, but I so desperately wanted a husband. I picked Joel to be that man, but he is incapable of being with just one woman. He is right; his father was the same way. His mother pushed his behavior to the side and ignored his unfaithfulness until the day they placed him in the grave.

So, I put on my oven mittens and took Joe's plate out of the oven and placed it on the table. I peeled back the aluminum foil and made sure to pour his favorite soft drink.

As he sat down to his meal, I mustered the courage to speak through my damaged feelings. "Joel, life is strange because one person's actions can trigger another person's actions. I have been living with a secret. It is time for us to be honest with each other, so let's do it." With those words, Joel rolled his eyes and said, "Woman, I am trying to enjoy my dinner. I am not up for a conversation, especially one that is probably based on a lie. Can I just enjoy my dinner and get some rest?"

"No, Joel," I said, "I need to get this off my chest. All those times that you flirted with other women, it damaged my ego. It made me feel inadequate and faulty. I know I should not depend on you for my self-worth, but I did. I wanted to be everything for you, but time after time, you proved to me that I am not, so I learned to live with that. But that is no way to live." Before I could continue, Joel interrupted me. "I swear I don't feel like hearing this tonight. Just pass me the bread, please. By the way, the red beans are very good, and this pork chop is cooked to perfection."

I countered, "Joel, I need you to listen to me for once in your life. I am trying to tell you that I have not been sitting back waiting for you to treat me the way I deserve to be treated. Over the past few weeks, I met a man who I found to be very nice and charming. He is not charming in the way you are, you know, flirtatious, but he is charming in a sexy way. He was interested in the things I like, and he actually listened to me when I talked. At first, I was uncomfortable with someone listening to my hopes and dreams because I was so used to you ignoring me."

At this point, Joel's eating started slowing down and eventually came to an end. He had this look on his face that I had never seen before. It was too late for me to stop my confession, so I decided to get it all out.

"Joel, I am not saying this to hurt you, but you want the freedom to see someone on the other side of town, and I should have the same freedom, don't you think?"

With those words, Joel picked up his plate of beans and threw it against the kitchen wall. With rage etched all over his face, he yelled out, "You whore! How could you do this to me? How could you be unfaithful? You're a woman, and this behavior is not expected from a woman. Did you sleep with this man?"

At first, I was afraid of Joel in this fit of rage because I had never seen him like this before. He was usually the most gregarious guy who kept a smile on his face, but I had dipped my toe into this pool of honesty, and it was too late to pull it out.

"Joel, of course I have slept with him. We're adults and we engaged in adult behaviors. Why would you ask me that?"

Joel was now pacing through the house. All I could hear was him crying and yelling at me, "You whore! You funky whore!"

I went into the kitchen to clean up the mess he made. I had some regret in my soul, but I also felt a sort of relief. I didn't want to hurt him because deep inside, I do have love for him, but I could not live the rest of my life consumed with Joel's unfaithful behavior. I deserve a life also.

Finally, I walked into the living room where Joel was now sitting on the sofa with his face buried in his hands. He was visibly upset, even crying. I was afraid to get near him or to speak and tell him that I didn't intend to hurt him, but I needed to be loved. I need to be loved in a way that didn't involve him loving other women. A feeling of empathy began to come over me, and as I approached him, Joel shot up and grabbed his jacket. He stormed out of the front door with such force that it cracked the glass on the door.

I walked out onto the porch and watched as Joel slipped into the night. I was unsure if I would ever see him again. Just as I turned to go back inside the house, Miss Alma was there on her porch. She shook her head and said, "You know, those walls that divide our house are paper-thin, and I could hear it all. I never took you for a woman who would step out on your Joel. I am not saying it was the best move because it probably cost you your marriage, but it was the smart move. No one, man or woman, should live in this world lonely for love. My late husband Harold did the same thing. He would hang out all night and come home at the crack of dawn. I told him the same thing, that I had met a man who made me smile and laugh. Just like your Joel,

Harold couldn't handle that news. He stayed away for months, and then one day I came outside to water my plants, and there he was sitting on the porch. We didn't talk about it much, but we made the best of the situation until the day I buried him. I can't promise you everything will work out, but I do know everything will be okay."

With those words, I headed inside and sat down to a plate of red beans and a fried pork chop. I had no idea what the future would hold, but I guess I will have to discover it.

Grits

Winter can be harsh, even in a place like New Orleans where we don't experience the harsh snow conditions, but instead, we get wet winters. Winter can be unforgiving when you have very little, and what little you do have, you spend it on keeping the heater running. Energy providers will cut off your heat without a second thought, and they don't care whether it's cold outside or inside. All they know is the bottom line, and the bottom line is paying your bill on time. Times have been tough lately, as one of my jobs closed down after Hurricane Katrina and never reopened. The extra money I used to earn from that job always covered my electricity costs, while my main job covered my rent and provided food. Times have been difficult, and there seems to be no indication of a brighter future.

I keep my head held high and my faith in God, but times are hard, and faith can sometimes waver. When it feels like I'm at the end of my rope, I hold on and pray, and it seems that God sees me through to the next day. I have so much to be thankful for amidst my lack, and I thank the Lord for His daily grace. My mother and sisters aren't doing well either; they decided to move in together to make ends meet. They've invited me to live with them, but the house is already crowded with them and their kids, and the last thing they need is another person in the house. My mother insists that I'm not a burden, and there's always room for family, but deep down inside, I know the last thing she needs is another person in her house.

Sometimes, when things are tight, and faith is fading, we have a way of returning to our roots to find our way through. I remember as a kid how my mother would have a pot of grits on the stove, and the aroma would wake me up in the morning. Even though my mother never talked about our financial situation, I knew that money wasn't abundant in our house. Grits were an economical way to keep our stomachs full and our minds focused on school rather than our circumstances. After years of eating grits every morning, I grew tired of the grain and began to complain to my mother. I wanted breakfast like the other families whose kids talked about cereal with milk and fruit. I wanted pancakes with hot syrup and crispy bacon strips. I wanted a breakfast and a life different from poverty, and I wanted it now.

That was my mindset as a child, and I didn't fully realize the extent of my mother's struggles as she raised us on her own. My father would occasionally come around, but it was usually in the early hours of the morning, and he would head straight to the bedroom with my mother. I was unaware of the difficulties my mother endured to feed us and provide us with clothes because she never revealed her struggles to us kids. I didn't understand that a breakfast of grits was better than no breakfast at all with a growling, empty stomach. I now recognize these things as I, too, am struggling to make ends meet in an economy that doesn't favor the poor or the middle class. I now see my mother as a saint for keeping our family together and ensuring we had food in our stomachs.

I wake up early in the morning to check the weather, determining whether I need two sweaters and a coat or just my coat. After assessing the conditions outside, I turn my attention to the contents of my cabinets. Once again, the cabinets are nearly bare, and I must consider what I can eat to sustain myself while I'm at work. I thank God for my job at a restaurant, as it provides me with a free lunch, which helps save money I don't actually have.

As I take one last look, I spot a container of grits. Memories flood back to me of days gone by, with grits for breakfast and my bad attitude about it. I reflect on how I complained about the food I didn't have and forgot to be thankful for the food I did have. I think of a mother who raised us without a full-time father at home and a father who used my mother as a brief stopover in his life. I think about how my sisters and I would sing songs at the breakfast table, with my mother joining in to keep our spirits high. I reminisce about a childhood where school lunch was a luxury, and other kids always seemed to have snacks while my stomach rumbled from hunger.

I reach into the cabinet and grab the container of grits, then put a pot of water on the stove. As I stir the grits in a clockwise motion, ensuring they don't stick to the bottom of the pot, I reflect on how grateful I should be to have breakfast. I look forward to a brighter day tomorrow and perhaps an additional job that will allow my cabinets to be filled with breakfast options. Until then, I will remain thankful for what I have and continue to face the winter weather to go to work.

While stirring the grits, I add a pat of butter and a dash of salt and pepper. I glance out of the kitchen window and see the children waiting at the bus stop, bundled up in their winter coats. I wonder if any of them had a breakfast like mine, just grits. I ponder whether they will appreciate their parents' efforts to make ends meet when those ends seem so far apart. As the grits are ready, I sit down to eat, bow my head, and thank God for what I have, trying not to dwell on what I lack. Today, I have grits for breakfast, and they taste wonderful.

Milton Keynes UK
Ingram Content Group UK Ltd.
UKHW030942071224
452128UK00010B/458

9 781977 278302